# Ma on the Oregon Trail

## The Johnsons Book 1

Bethany Hauck

# Copywrite

# Characters

Johnson Family:

George Johnson-Father
Rose Johnson-Mother
John Johnson-Grandfather
Victoria Johnson-Grandmother

Children:
Kenny-24
Henry-20
Lily-18
Michelle-15
Eddie-13

Sadie Mills-Engaged to Kenny
Jeremiah Smith-Engaged to Lily
Nick Garrett-Kenny's best friend

Wagon Train:
Norman and Nellie Fisher
Callie Fisher-their daughter
Harley Shepard-Wagon Train Leader
Reverend Drews and his wife Julia Drews
Dr. Martin

# Table of Contents

# Chapter 1. Going West

Kenny Johnson looked around the large table where his family sat eating their Sunday supper. Sharing the meal were his parents, his Grandma and Grandpa Johnson, his two younger sisters, Lily and Michelle, and two younger brothers, Henry and Eddie. Also joining them were his sister Lily's fiance, Jeremiah Smith, and his fiance, Sadie Mills. He knew what he was going to say wasn't going to make his mother happy, but it was time to tell them all his and Sadie's plan.

He glanced over at Sadie who gave him a small nod and smile. "Sadie and I have something to tell you," Kenny said to his family, getting everyone's attention.

"What is it, son?" George Johnson, Kenny's dad, asked. "Are you changing the date of the wedding?"

"No," Kenny answered, "the wedding date won't change. We've only got one more month to go; I can wait."

"Well spit it out, boy," John Johnson, Kenny's grandpa said.

"We've decided that after the wedding, we're going to join a wagon train and head out west to Oregon," Kenny said as his family sat looking at him, not knowing how to respond.

"Why?" Rose Johnson, his mama, finally asked.

"Because war between the states is coming, Mama," Kenny told her. "I've listened to what the people in town are saying, and I don't want to be here in Kentucky when it starts, and have to pick a side to fight on."

"I can understand that," his father told him, "I'm not liking some of the talk I hear in town, people are already beginning to argue. What do you plan on doing out there?"

"There's some good land in Oregon," Kenny told them. "Me and Sadie heard about this place called the Willamette Valley. I've got my eye on a piece of land there; we're going to raise cattle."

"Can I go?" Kenny's twenty-year-old brother, Henry, asked suddenly, making Rose gasp. "I don't want to leave Paducah, but I agree, war is coming."

"You can," Kenny said, nodding at him. "If you've got enough money, it might be a good idea for you to have your own wagon and supplies."

"I understand why you want to go," Rose told her two sons, trying not to show her sadness, "I don't want to see either of you go off to war, but I'll worry about the three of you so far away all alone."

"We won't be alone, Mama," Kenny assured her. "Nick's going too; he's just leaving a month or so after us."

"Nick Garrett?" his eighteen-year-old sister Lily asked, a scowl on her face. "Why isn't he just going with you?"

"He has a buyer for his farm, but they can't pay him until the end of March," Kenny explained. "We'll be leaving the first week of March for Missouri."

"Can't you wait for him?" Rose asked. "Wouldn't it be better for all of you to travel together?"

"We've already been accepted into our wagon train," Kenny explained. "I've already got a wagon, oxen and supplies ordered, and it'll be waiting for us in Independence. Our wagon train leaves there in the middle of April. It'll be too difficult to change everything now."

6

"You sure you want to go, Henry?" George asked his second oldest. "I hear it's a difficult journey."

"I know I don't want to fight in a war that I'm not sure I believe in," Henry told his parents. "I'd rather take my chances on the trail. I'm sure I'll be fine with Kenny and Sadie."

"Nick's looking to buy the land right next to mine. We're going to try ranching together to start."

"What about me?" Henry asked.

"I remember there being quite a few pieces of property that connected to the one I want that were still available," Kenny answered. "We can go down to the land office and look tomorrow if you want, or you can live with Sadie and me until you're ready for a house of your own."

"I'll have to see how much money I've got put away in the bank," Henry told him. "I'm not sure if I've got enough saved for the wagon, supplies and land."

"If you're sure you want to go," George interrupted, "then I'll make sure you've got the funds to buy what you need."

"Thank you, Papa," Henry said.

"You're awful quiet, Sadie," Victoria Johnson, Kenny's grandma, said. "How do you feel about all this, dear?"

"Leaving home and my family is scary," Sadie answered, "but the idea of Kenny going to war and possibly not coming back, is even scarier."

"Oregon is a state now," John said.

"I know, Grandpa," Kenny replied, "and a free state. That's part of why we want to go there."

"Well I think you're all crazy," Jeremiah said, "Lily and I'll be staying right here in Kentucky after our wedding. With you both gone, your Papa and Grandpa will need some help on the farm."

"I'm glad to hear that," George said nodding. "I'd hate for my daughter to be traveling that far from home. You're right Jeremiah; we'll need some help around here until Eddie's old enough to take over."

"I want to go to Oregon too," thirteen-year-old Eddie, the youngest of the Johnson children, said.

"Not for a few years yet, young man," Rose told him, making him frown. "How did your parents take the news, Sadie?"

"Mama was upset at first," Sadie answered, "but she understands why we need to go. Her and Papa traveled to Kentucky in a wagon from Virginia over twenty years ago."

"She's told me that story," Rose said.

"Mama said if she was younger, she'd make Papa pack up the farm and come with us," Sadie told them. "They don't know what they're going to do if the war comes to Paducah."

"I'm a bit worried about that myself," George admitted. "But I'm too old to be packing up and leaving."

"Nothing's going to happen," Jeremiah said, "everyone is panicking for nothing."

"I wish I felt as sure of that as you," George said and most of the other Johnson's nodded their agreement.

"How are you gonna to get to Independence if you're not buying your wagon till you get there?" Eddie asked.

"We'll take the small wagon and team I own now," Kenny explained. "I've agreed to trade them in toward the price of the wagon and oxen."

"Oxen?" Eddie asked.

"That's what they recommend using to get all the way to Oregon," Kenny told him. "The trails to hard for horses."

"You're leaving the first week of March?" George asked. "Where are you going to sleep? It'll still be pretty cold at night."

8

"It's four-hundred miles to Independence, Papa," Kenny told him. "We have to get there, pick up our wagon and supplies, get everything organized, and be ready to leave on April twentieth. I'm hoping to make ten miles a day. I should be able to; the roads are well traveled all the way there."

"You should be able to make fifteen to twenty," John said, "but it's good to give yourself extra time."

"I think so too, Grandpa," Kenny said.

"Well, son," George said, "I'll be sad to see you all leave, but I'll be waiting anxiously for your letters."

"I'll make sure they write, Papa Johnson," Sadie assured him.

"Look," Victoria said, pointing towards the window, "it's beginning to snow. We should be getting back to our cabin before the road gets slick, John."

"I agree," John told his wife. "If no one needs anything else from us, we'll be taking our leave."

"Be careful," George said to his parents who nodded as they put their coats on.

"We promised Sadie's parents we'd bring her home after supper," Rose reminded George.

"That we did," George answered, "we'll take her as soon as we finish helping you clean up, the roads shouldn't be too slippery yet."

"Can I go?" Eddie asked.

"Of course," George answered. "We can all go if you'd like."

"You go ahead and take Mama, Papa," Lily told her father, "I'll stay here, clean up and do the dishes."

"I'd appreciate that, Lily," Rose said, patting her daughter's hand.

"I'll stay and help," Michelle, who was fifteen and had sat quietly listening to everyone else, added.

"Look what thoughtful daughters we've raised, George," Rose said, smiling at her two girls.

"I think I should be getting home myself," Jeremiah told them. "You know how slippery the roads become with just a little snow."

"I'll walk you out," Lily said.

"No need for you to come out and get chilled," Jeremiah told her, "I'm going to make a trip to the outhouse before I leave anyway."

"Then safe travels," Lily said to him as he squeezed her hand and smiled at her.

"Yes," Victoria said as he walked towards the door, "safe travels." She'd never really warmed up to the young man. She pulled open the door and said, "Come on, John, help this old woman get home."

"Old?" John joked, "don't be calling my bride old. She's still the most beautiful woman I've ever laid eyes on." Everyone laughed as he followed her out the door with Jeremiah right behind.

"Are you boys going to ride with us?" George asked Kenny and Henry as the rest of the family began stacking the dishes.

"I'll be staying home. I've got some chores to finish around here," Henry answered. "Did you milk the cows, Eddie?"

"I forgot," Eddie said.

"You'll have to stay home then," George told him. "You know chores have to be done before anything else."

"If Sadie doesn't mind," Kenny said, "I'll stay here and help Eddie. He was helping me chop some wood before dinner, that's why he didn't get the milking done."

10

"I don't mind," Sadie said to him. "It'll be nice for your Mama and Papa to ride back just the two of them. A romantic winter wagon ride."

"Oh stop," Rose said and blushed while everyone else, except Eddie, began to laugh.

"Go ahead, Mama," Henry teased, "enjoy your time with Papa. I bet he even tries to steal a kiss or two."

"You're right about that," George said, leaning over and kissing his wife on the cheek.

"You old fool," Rose said as she pushed him away, but she was laughing.

**********

"Don't you think Mama and Papa should've been back by now?" Lily asked her two older brothers.

"Maybe they stopped to visit with someone," Kenny said.

"They're probably just enjoying spending time alone," Henry added. "They don't get to do that very often."

"Do you think Grandma and Grandpa made it home?" Eddie asked as he came in from his chores out in the barn. "It's getting awfully slippery out there."

"They did," Michelle answered. "Henry walked over and made sure. At least they didn't have to go far."

"That house we helped Papa build on the edge of the property is perfect for them," Kenny said.

"It is," Henry agreed, "Grandpa's getting too old to be doing farm work every day. If he was here and saw us working, he'd insist on helping."

"We'll be building our own houses come the end of the year," Kenny said to Henry. "I'm glad Papa showed us how."

11

"I think I'd like a house of my own once there's time," Henry said. "A log cabin would be good to enough for me. I don't want to be in your and Sadie's way."

"You won't be," Kenny assured him, "but we'll get you a house built as soon as we can."

"I like that Grandma and Grandpa still live close," Michelle said, "I'm so used to seeing Grandma every day, I'd miss her if I didn't."

"Me too," Lily added. "I'm going to miss my big brothers though."

"You'll be so busy planning your wedding in the fall, you won't have time to miss us," Kenny said to her.

"I can't believe you're not going to be here for my wedding," Lily said sadly.

"I'm sorry, Lily," Kenny told her, "but the ideal time to leave for Oregon is mid-April to mid-May. If you want to move your wedding up, then we'll be there."

"No," Lily quickly said, "Jeremiah and I need more time before we wed. We're both still getting used to the idea."

"I can't wait to marry Sadie," Kenny told them, "I've known since I was ten-years-old that she was the girl I was going to marry."

"And it took you fourteen years to work up the courage to ask her?" Lily teased, and Kenny nodded and grinned. Henry and Michelle burst out laughing.

"That sounds like the wagon now," Henry said as they heard the familiar sound coming down the road.

"Papa seems to be driving fast," Kenny commented, becoming concerned

"He does," Lily agreed, she started heading for the door with Kenny right behind. "I hope nothing's wrong."

They exited the house and watched as a wagon traveled towards them, much to fast on the snow-slickened trail. They watched as not their parents, but Sadie's pulled up in front of the cabin. Both looked very upset.

"Mr. and Mrs. Mills," Kenny said, going to greet them and helping Sadie's mama down. "Mama and Papa were supposed to bring Sadie home. They left quite a while ago."

"Come in the house, Kenny," Mr. Mills said. "We've got some news." He took his wife by the arm and lead her towards the door where Eddie stood peeking out.

"What is it?" Kenny asked as soon as he shut the door behind them. "Is Sadie alright?"

"I don't even know how to tell you this," Mr. Mills started, his voice breaking. "There was an accident on the road just outside of town. Somehow some of the spokes snapped on your Papa's wagon wheel, which caused the wheel to break and come off. The wagon tipped over into the ravine next to it. No one survived."

"Mama and Papa?" Lily asked, falling into a seat.

"They're gone," Mr. Mills said.

"Sadie?" Kenny asked, stunned.

"Our daughter is also gone," Mr. Mills said as he too plopped down on one of the chairs around the large table and began to cry.

**\*\*\*\*\*\*\*\*\*\***

"...and we commit their bodies to the ground: earth to earth, ashes to ashes, dust to dust. The Lord bless them and keep them, the Lord make His Face to shine upon them and be gracious to them, the Lord lift up His countenance upon them and give them peace. Amen." The minister from the church looked up at the five Johnson children and Mr. and Mrs. Mills as he concluded the funeral. "Would any of you like to say something?" he asked them.

"No," they all answered together. What more was there to say?

Their lives the last two days had been filled with making arrangements and consoling each other. Kenny knew now that the funeral was over, it was time to make some decisions. He was the oldest, and it was up to him to look out for his younger brothers and sisters. He planned on talking to all of them once they got back to the house and read the will his parents had left in case anything ever happened to them.

Kenny was numb as he stood and shook the hands of the friends and family who showed up for the combined funeral. He was glad that the Mills' agreed to it; he didn't think he could have done this twice. He looked around at his siblings and grandparents to see how they were holding up.

Grandma and Grandpa were sad, but being strong. Thankfully, most of his aunts, uncles and cousins showed up the night before, which eased his Grandma's heart just a little.

Lily was leaning on Jeremiah for support. He'd shown up early yesterday morning and hadn't left Lily's side except to go home and sleep. Kenny had never really liked Jeremiah; he'd always hoped Lily and Nick would end up together. He had to give Jeremiah credit though for supporting Lily.

Henry and Michelle were very quiet. They both seemed to just want to get the day over with. Kenny hoped his brother still planned to go with him out west. In fact, he had plans for all of them.

Eddie was in the worst shape. He'd barely stopped crying since they'd gotten word about the accident. Kenny hoped the adventure he was going to offer him would help him go on. He was hoping the same for himself.

Once the last of the guests left the cemetery they headed back to the house they'd all grown up in. Grandma and Grandpa Johnson, the aunts and uncles, and all the cousins sat around and told stories about Sadie Mills, and George and Rose Johnson, until it was almost dark. Soon after that, everyone took their leave. Finally, it was just the five Johnson's, their grandparents, and Jeremiah left. Kenny took a deep breath, before pulling out the will.

"Before I open this," Kenny said, "I'd like to make a proposal to all of you."

"What is it?" Michelle asked.

"No matter what this says, let's go west, to Oregon," he said, "all of us."

"You don't mean your Grandma and me too, do ya, boy?" his grandpa asked.

"All of us," Kenny said. "You could do it, Grandpa, and we'd all do as much as we could to make the trip easier on Grandma."

"I'm not worried about your grandma, boy," John told his grandson, "she's as strong as the day I married her, but we can't go."

"We've still got other children and grandchildren here, Kenny," his grandma said. "If I was just a bit younger though, I'd jump at the chance to go."

"You would, wouldn't you?" his grandpa said to her, and although he was exhausted after burying his son and daughter-in-law, he still looked at her the same way he did when he'd married her more than forty years earlier.

"Adventure is good," Victoria told him. "It keeps you young. I'm a bit worried myself about what's going to happen if war breaks out. Some of our family will be on one side, and some on the other."

"Read the will, Kenny," Lily said sadly. She already knew she was going to turn down the trip out west, Jeremiah had told her more than once how foolish her brothers were being.

"They left the farm and money at the bank to me," Kenny said after reading for a few minutes. "I'm to either keep it, or sell it, but the two acres Grandma and Grandpa's cabin is on will remain in Grandpa's name."

"What about the rest of us?" Michelle asked.

"If I keep the farm, you're to be able to live on it for as long as you like," Kenny said, "but if I sell, Lily and Michelle each get one-hundred dollars, Henry and Eddie each get one-thousand dollars."

"That doesn't seem fair," Jeremiah said, "shouldn't the farm be split five ways if you're leaving anyway?"

"It's how our families always done it," Grandpa said. "I passed the land down to my oldest son, who is passing it down to his oldest son. The boys get a bigger portion because they'll need to buy land of their own. The girls will have a small amount of money to take with them into their marriage."

"I was planning on moving here to help with the chores anyway after you left and Lily and I married," Jeremiah said, "I'd be happy to keep the farm going for you after you leave."

"I'm going to sell it," Kenny said, making a decision. "I'd like Michelle and Eddie to come to Oregon with me and Henry. You too, Lily."

16

"I can't go," Lily said, looking over at Jeremiah who was already shaking his head no, an angry look on his face. "Jeremiah doesn't want to."

"You don't need to sound so disappointed, Lily. If you want to go with your brothers and get yourselves killed, don't let me stop you," Jeremiah said. He stomped across the room over to the door and left.

"I don't know what you see in him," Henry said.

"He's actually really sweet at times," Lily said, defending him.

"Come on, Lily," Eddie said, "come with us."

"You want to go?" Lily asked.

"Yes," Eddie said, "I don't want to live in this house anymore. It makes me miss Mama and Papa."

"We all miss them," Michelle said, putting her arm around him, "but I agree with you. I don't want to stay in this house; I'll go."

They all turned and looked at Lily, "I can't," she said again, struggling with her decision to stay.

"Come on, Lily," Kenny said it this time. "I'll take the money from the farm and buy more land. That way when you and Michelle marry, you can stay near us."

"I'm going to stay and marry Jeremiah," Lily said quietly.

"Lily can stay with us until her wedding," Rose told her other grandchildren. "She'll be fine with us; you do what you need to."

"You're sure, Lily?" Kenny asked one more time.

"I'm sure," Lily answered, even though she wasn't.

\*\*\*\*\*\*\*\*\*\*

"I'd always hoped you and Lily would end up marrying," Kenny said to Nick as they left the land office a week later.

17

"I think we were heading that way until I screwed it up," Nick said.

"What do you mean?" Henry asked.

"You never did tell me what you did," Kenny said to his best friend. "One day the two of you were courting, and the next she would barely even talk to you."

"I've never told anyone what happened," Nick said, "just know that it was my fault. I screwed everything up."

"You're still not going to tell me?" Kenny asked. "I wish I felt better about Jeremiah. I keep telling myself I dislike him so much because he isn't you."

"Every time I see him with her, I just want to punch him," Nick admitted. "He sure moved in quick once the two of us split."

"That he did," Kenny said. "I thought for sure you'd get back together. You really won't tell me what happened?"

Nick thought about it for a minute before speaking. "Remember at the end of summer when we all went to the Harvest Festival at the church?" Nick asked.

"Of course," Kenny said, "that's the last night the two of you were together."

"Yes, it was," Nick said. "I was standing in the corner watching the dancing when Beth Hanson found me. I thought it was your sister trying to steal a kiss, but it wasn't. By the time I realized who it was, your sister saw Beth kissing me. Lily stormed out of the church, and I chased after her. We had a terrible argument."

"Did you explain what happened?" Kenny asked.

"I tried," Nick said, "but she wouldn't listen."

"I'm surprised she didn't calm down in a day or two," Henry said.

18

"She might have," Nick said, "but she used some very bad language, which I warned her about. Then she used the same language again."

"What kind of language?" Kenny asked.

"She said I was a two-timing bastard and she hoped I burned in hell," Nick said.

"Papa would have taken a strap to her for that," Kenny said.

"I used my hand," Nick said quietly.

"You spanked Lily?" Kenny asked, not sure if he should be angry or laugh.

"I did," Nick said, "and I don't regret it. No wife of mine is going to use language like that. I showed her what will happen every time words like that leave her lips."

"You're lucky my Papa never found out," Henry told him, "he would have made you marry her after that."

"I wish he would have then," Nick said sadly.

"I don't know if I should hug you or hit you," Henry said, hiding his grin.

"I prefer you do neither," Nick admitted. "I lost Lily that day, but maybe it's for the best. Maybe we didn't suit as much as I thought we did."

"I still wish it was you marrying her," Kenny said.

"Me too," Henry added. "I'll miss her when we're in Oregon."

"So will I," Kenny said.

"I've missed her every day since the Harvest Festival," Nick told them both. "It's one of the reasons I'm willing to sell my farm and go to Oregon."

# Chapter 2. Independence

"I'm going to miss you so much," Lily said to her brothers and sister, as they loaded up the small wagon with as many of their belongings as they could fit for the trip to Independence, Missouri.

"We don't leave Independence until the middle of April," Kenny told her for the third time that day, as he gave her one last hug, "if you decide to come, you need to be there before then."

"I know," Lily said as she stepped back beside her grandparents, "but I can't go."

"I wish you'd change your mind," Kenny said as Lily looked at him sadly and shook her head.

"You all be careful," John said to the rest of his grandchildren as he put his arm around Lily, "I hear the trail is a dangerous place, but worth it in the end."

"I hope so, Grandpa," Henry said as he hugged Lily and his Grandma one last time before climbing up onto the wagon bench and taking the reins. "We'll send a telegram when we get to Independence, and a letter from Fort Laramie."

"We'll be looking for them," Rose said as she hugged Eddie one last time. "You listen to your brothers now, you hear?"

"I will, Grandma," Eddie said as he climbed into the back of the wagon next to Michelle.

"You can send letters whenever you want to Oregon City. That's where we'll be stopping for a few days before heading to our land. They'll beat us there, but we'll pick them up as soon as we get off the trail. We'll keep Eddie and Michelle safe," Kenny assured them all as he climbed up next to Henry. He looked back one last time at his sister and grandparents, wondering if he'd ever see them again as they rode down the road to their new adventure.

"How long will it take us to get to Independence?" Eddie asked from behind them a short time later.

"About a month," Kenny answered.

"Where will we sleep?" Eddie asked.

"Didn't we already talk about this?" Henry asked.

"I just want to hear it again," Eddie said to them, making Kenny and Henry both smile.

"We'll camp out under the stars most nights," Kenny explained, "but we can get rooms in hotels if there's a town around."

"What about in Independence?" Eddie asked.

"We'll stay in a hotel while we get our wagon, team and supplies together. Once we've got it, we'll move out across the river to where the wagons are being assembled and stay there. Once we leave for Oregon, the wagons will be our new home," Kenny told him.

"You still want to get two wagons?" Henry asked.

"I do," Kenny told him. "We can teach Eddie and Michelle how to drive them to give us a rest at times. That way if one wagon breaks, we'll have another. We can also take twice the supplies."

"I think it's a good plan," Henry said, "we've got plenty of money from selling the homestead."

"We do," Kenny agreed, "and all of our land claims in Oregon are paid for already. Once Nick get there, we'll have over two thousand acres between us."

"I'm getting excited," Henry admitted, "I feel like Eddie when it's almost Christmas."

"Me too, little brother," Kenny said.

"Do you think Lily will be alright?" Michelle asked them.

"Grandma and Grandpa will keep watch on her," Kenny assured her.

"And Jeremiah," Eddie added.

"Yes," Kenny said tentatively, "and Jeremiah."

**********

"It's cold today," Michelle said from the back of the wagon.

"It is," Kenny answered. "We're over half way to Independence though. There are some extra blankets in a trunk back there. Get one out and cover yourself up, we don't need anyone catching a chill and getting sick."

"Do you think it'll be this cold on the Oregon Trail?" Eddie asked as he wrapped one of his Mama's quilts around him.

"I heard that when we first start out of Missouri, it can get pretty cold at night," Henry said to them. He'd been reading everything he could get his hands on about the trek across the country. "Then once summer comes and we're on the plains, we'll have to battle the heat. There aren't a lot of trees out there to shade us. Once we get to the Rocky Mountains, the weather can be quite cool up there again until we get across."

"I can handle the cold and hot," Kenny said to all of them, "I'm just hoping we can avoid some of the storms I've heard about."

"I read a bit about them," Henry said, "some said they saw hail as round as a cannonball, and winds that blew so hard they ripped trees right out of the ground."

"I think I'm more worried about the Indians," Michelle said.

22

"From what I read, if you leave them alone, they usually leave you alone," Henry told her, "just don't be wandering away from the wagon once we're out on the plains."

"We're well ahead of schedule," Kenny said, "how would you all feel about stopping in Columbia for a few nights?"

"I've never heard of it," Eddie said.

"A man in St. Louis said it's a city about halfway between St. Louis and Independence," Kenny told him. "We can stay for a night or two if everyone wants."

"I want to," Michelle said, "I'm tired of being in this wagon all day."

"Get used to it, Michelle," Kenny said to her, "you'll be traveling in the wagon all day every day soon, there won't be any other choice."

"Not true," Henry said, "I read that the lighter the load, the longer the oxen last, and the further you travel each day. Most people walk behind the wagons."

"We're going to walk all the way to Oregon?" Eddie asked.

"Most of the way," Henry told him and laughed at the look on Michelle's face.

"How long does it take to get there?" Eddie asked.

"Five or six months," Kenny told him. "Depends on the weather we run into and how well the train works together."

"Look," Eddie said suddenly pointing way down the road in front of them. "That looks like another wagon."

"I wonder why they're just sitting there?" Kenny asked.

"Only one way to find out," Henry answered.

When they arrived at the wagon, they pulled in behind it. A man and his wife were working on the cover which must've blown partially off.

"Hello there," Kenny called to them, "do you need some help?"

"Well howdy," the man and his wife stopped what they were doing and turned towards Kenny. "I think we've just about got it, the damn rope broke, but thanks for the offer."

"Norman, watch your language," the woman scolded.

"You folks headed to Independence?" Henry asked them, smothering back his grin.

"We are," the man answered. "I'm Norman Fisher, and this is my wife, Nellie."

"Nice to meet you, Norman and Nellie. I'm Kenny Johnson, and these are my brothers, Henry and Eddie, and this young lady is my sister, Michelle."

"You folks heading west too?" Norman asked.

"We are," Kenny answered. "Our wagon train is supposed to leave Independence on April twentieth."

"Your train being led by Harley Shepard?" Norman asked.

"It is," Kenny answered.

"Us too," Norman said, "we'll be traveling together."

"Then I'm glad we met," Kenny said. "You sure you don't need any help?"

"No," Norman said. "We'll secure it well enough to get us to Columbia. We're ahead of schedule, so maybe we can stay a night or two there and fix it proper."

"We were planning on stopping there too," Henry said, "would the two of you be willing to join us for a meal at a restaurant there this evening?"

"There's actually three of us," Nellie said, "our daughter Callie is around here somewhere."

"She just wandered off?" Kenny asked frowning.

"She's not happy about this move out west," Norman explained. "She makes sure we don't forget that."

"So she's pouting," Kenny said to them.

"Pretty much," Norman said.

"There's a sure-fire cure for that," Kenny mumbled, thinking of how his papa handled pouting.

"If you'd be interested, we could travel to Independence together," Michelle said hopefully from the back of the wagon; she loved her brothers, but it'd be nice to travel with other women.

"You plan on taking that little wagon all the way to Oregon?" Norman asked them.

"No, sir," Henry answered, "we've got two prairie schooners waiting for us in Independence, plus supplies and oxen."

"Thank goodness," Nellie said, "I was afraid you were going to try and travel in that small wagon. You'd never make it."

"Where you folks from?" Kenny asked.

"North Carolina," Norman answered, "we've been traveling for over a month already."

Just then their daughter Callie came walking back to the wagon. Kenny watched as she walked passed her parents without even saying hello. He figured she must have been about the same age as Lily, maybe a year older at most. He noticed right away what a beauty she was.

"Say howdy to the Johnsons, Callie," Norman said, stopping her.

"Howdy," Callie turned and said politely, but she didn't smile.

"Howdy, ma'am," Kenny said to her. Callie nodded at him, walked to the back of the wagon and climbed inside.

"She's not usually so rude," Nellie tried to explain, "we're hoping she gets used to the idea before we leave Independence."

25

"Why doesn't she want to go?" Eddie asked. "I'm glad to be leaving, our Mama and Papa died, and I don't want to live at our house anymore."

"I'm sorry to hear that, son," Norman said. "Sometimes change is good. We sold our farm in North Carolina. Wars coming, I can feel it. I don't want to be anywhere near here when it happens."

"I feel the same way, Norman," Kenny admitted. "Let us help you get your wagon fixed, and we can travel together to Columbia if that sounds alright to you."

"Sounds good, Kenny," Norman said, "I knew we'd find good people on this trip."

\*\*\*\*\*\*\*\*\*\*

"Why don't you want to go to Oregon, Callie?" Kenny asked the girl sitting next to him. Poor Norman had come down with a horrible head cold and cough. So he could rest, Henry offered to drive his wagon with Nellie. Norman felt poorly enough that he'd agreed. Instead of sitting in the back of the wagon with her Papa, Callie decided to ride with the Johnsons.

"I had lots of friends in North Carolina," Callie told him. "I've never lived anywhere else and liked my life there. If Mama and Papa could've waited another year or two, I could've stayed."

"What do you mean?" Kenny asked.

"I'll be twenty in the beginning of May," she answered. "I'm sure in a year or more, I would've been married, there were a few men interested."

"I'm sure there were," Kenny said, surprised that the idea of other men looking at her bothered him. "You would have let your parents go to Oregon without you?" Kenny asked.

"Weren't you going to go without your parents?" Callie asked.

"I was," Kenny said, "but I would have missed them terribly."

"I would have too," Callie admitted, "but I still would've stayed in North Carolina."

"You aren't worried about a war happening?" Kenny asked.

"That's silly talk," Callie said, "there isn't going to be any war."

"There is, Callie," Kenny said, "that's all anyone seems to talk about. If this Abe Lincoln fella from Illinois gets elected, there's gonna be a war. Who knows where it'll be fought, or which side some of the states will choose to fight on."

"You sound like my Papa," Callie said. "The only difference between the two of you is that he ruined my life because of his silly beliefs. We don't even know who's going to be running for president yet. The election is still over a year away."

"Your Papa's not being silly, he's right," Kenny said. "Instead of being mad at him, you should be thanking him for getting you out of there before it happens. There's too many differences right now between the north states and the south."

"The states will work out their problems like they always have. I'll never thank Papa for making me leave," Callie said.

"Well, I have to tell you, I don't like how you treat your parents," Kenny said.

"It has nothing to do with you," Callie said.

"I just lost my parents, Callie," Kenny told her. "I'd give anything to talk to them again, and you ignore yours. How long you planning to keep that up?"

"All the way to Oregon," Callie said.

"My papa would have put Lily or Michelle over his knee until they agreed to change their attitude. Norman needs to do the same to you," Kenny said to her.

"He wouldn't dare," Callie said, "and I wouldn't let him."

"My Papa wouldn't have asked," Kenny told her, "and if you want my opinion, that's exactly what you deserve."

"Then I don't want your opinion," Callie said.

"Maybe I'll turn you over my knee myself," Kenny threatened, becoming irritated with her attitude.

"You wouldn't dare," Callie said.

"Treat your Mama or Papa like you have been one more time in front of me," Kenny said, "and you may not like the consequences."

"My Papa would never allow it," Callie told him.

"Then maybe your Papa doesn't need to know," Kenny mumbled.

**********

"Is that it?" Eddie said, pointing towards the large town that just came into view.

"That's it," Kenny answered, "Independence, Missouri."

"When do we leave for Oregon?" Michelle asked.

"We've got a week," Kenny answered.

"What'll we do for the next week while we wait?" Michelle asked.

"There's plenty to do," Kenny told her. "We gotta pick up the wagons and oxen, learn how to put them on the yolks and take them off, pick up our supplies and pack the wagons, and then me and Henry are going to teach you and Eddie how to drive the teams."

"You'll let me?" Michelle asked.

28

"When we're on the plains it shouldn't be too hard," Kenny said, "I think you can do it."

"Of course I can," Michelle said, "it can't be that much harder than driving the wagon with horses back home."

"I think it's going to be very different," Kenny said, "oxen are much stronger than horses, and not as smart."

"Are we still going to sleep in the wagons?" Eddie asked.

"Tonight we can get rooms at one of the hotels. I'm sure we can find one. We'll order everyone a hot bath and supper too," Kenny told him.

"I don't need a bath," Eddie said, "I swam in the creek with Henry where we stopped last night."

"You'll be taking a bath," Kenny assured him, "if you think you need one or not, understand?"

"I guess," Eddie answered; the disappointment in his voice made both Kenny and Michelle grin.

"We might not get another one for a long time," Michelle told him, "I for one, plan on soaking until my fingers wrinkle."

"You're such a girl, Michelle," Eddie said disapprovingly.

The three sat silently as they rode toward the town. Henry was still driving the Fisher's wagon since Norman was just beginning to feel better. Callie was riding on the bench with him while Nellie sat in the back keeping Norman company.

"How come Callie hasn't been riding with us the last few days?" Michelle asked.

"She didn't like some of the things I said to her," Kenny answered honestly.

"What did you say?" Eddie asked, then added, "I like Callie, she's nice to me."

"She's nice to everyone except her Mama and Papa," Kenny told his brother and sister, "and that's a problem. I told her

29

if she treated our Mama or Papa like that, she would have ended up over Papa's knee."

"She would have," Michelle said, "I'm surprised her Papa hasn't done it himself."

"From what she told me," Kenny explained, "he never has."

"Papa took a belt to me once," Eddie said, thinking back.

"What did you do?" Kenny asked.

"I was out playing with the Millers. We lost track of time, and I didn't come home until after dark. Mama was worried about me."

"I remember that day," Michelle said. "Papa took you out to the woodshed."

"He did," Eddie said, then grinned as he rubbed his butt, remembering the belting.

"I bet it couldn't have hurt as much as Mama's hairbrush," Michelle said and giggled. "Once me and Lily found a rattler out in the garden. Instead of going and getting Papa right away, we threw rocks at it so that it would rattle its tail. When Mama came out and seen us messing with that snake, she took her hairbrush to both of us."

"Sounds like Mama," Kenny said, he was grinning too. "She took a switch to me and Henry once. That hurt like the dickens for two days after."

"What did you do?" Eddie asked.

"We went out riding and decided to practice rounding up cattle with Mr. Waters stock."

"That doesn't sound too bad," Michelle said.

"It wasn't," Kenny said, then chuckled and added, "until we made his herd stampede, and they broke through the fence and just missed his cabin as they charged by."

"And Mama switched you? Not Papa?" Michelle asked.

"Both," Kenny said and laughed. "Mama took a switch to us right after Mr. Waters left. Then she made us stand in the corners of the barn until Papa got home. He took his belt to us after. We could have killed someone."

"I miss them so much," Michelle said, and a tear rolled down her cheek.

"We all do," Kenny said to her, patting her hand on the wagon bench next to him. "Oregon will be a new start for us all."

"Do you think we'll make it?" Michelle asked.

"We'll make it," Kenny told her, "we've got to."

"I miss Lily," Eddie said.

"We all do," Kenny said again.

**********

"Did they have any rooms?" Nellie asked as Kenny and Norman came back out of the hotel.

"They did," Norman said, "but only three rooms were left. We took them all for the next two nights."

"I'm not staying in a room with you and Mama," Callie said to her papa.

"Behave, Callie," Norman warned, "you don't have to. You'll be sharing a room with Michelle."

Callie cheered up immediately. "We'll have so much fun," she said to Michelle.

"You'll both need to be getting to sleep early," Kenny told them. "Remember, we've got lots of work to do the next few days, Michelle."

"Where am I sleeping?" Eddie asked.

"With me and Henry," Kenny told him, "they said they could set up a cot in the room for one of us, the other two will have to share the bed."

"I'll take the cot," Eddie said quickly.

"I don't think so, squirt," Henry said laughing. "You're stuck with one of us in the bed."

"Sometimes it stinks being the smallest," Eddie said, and Henry ruffled his hair.

"Let's get this stuff unloaded, put away in our rooms and grab a hot meal in the hotel restaurant," Norman said, "now that I'm feeling better, I'm starving."

"Sounds good, Norman," Kenny said, "I think we'll enjoy a meal and then maybe take a quick stroll around the town before calling it a night. The work can wait until the morning."

**********

"What were they saying in North Carolina? Do they think this Lincoln fella might run and win the election?" Kenny asked Norman as the Johnsons and Fishers ate supper together.

"It depends on what part of North Carolina you're in," Norman explained. "The area we're from doesn't have any of those large plantations, or many slaves. Most people there wouldn't mind seeing slavery end. If you go east where the larger cities and plantations are at, then they say if Lincoln does run and win, they don't want to be part of the United States anymore."

"The same for us in Kentucky," Kenny told him. "Some people are for keeping slaves and some against."

"Papa always said one man shouldn't be able to own another," Eddie said.

"Your Papa sounds like a smart man," Norman said to Eddie. "I feel the same."

"The problem is even people in our own family are split on the issue," Henry said, "if war comes, some of the cousins will be fighting on one side, while the rest fight on the other."

"That would be hard," Norman said as he finished his meal. "I think all North Carolinians will fight for the south, no matter how they feel about slavery."

"That was a great meal," Kenny said wiping his mouth, "we need to enjoy it while we can. We'll be eating Michelle's cooking until we get to Oregon."

"My cooking isn't that bad," Michelle protested, then grinned when she realized Kenny was teasing.

"Don't worry, Michelle," Nellie told her, "Callie and I'll help you. It might be easier if we just cook one big meal for both families, if everyone agrees."

"I'd agree with that," Kenny said; Henry and Eddie nodded.

"I've never cooked over a campfire," Callie said.

"You'll learn," Nellie told her, "if you would've come out of the wagon on the trip here, you could've learned how to already."

"I shouldn't have to learn," Callie said to her mother, "I should still be with my friends in North Carolina, cooking over the stove in our home."

"Callie," Norman said, "I'm getting real tired of explaining to you why we needed to leave."

"It doesn't matter now anyway, Papa," Callie said, crossing her arms over her chest, "it's too late to take me back."

"I wouldn't have taken you back anyway," Norman said. "Once we get to Oregon you'll find new friends and happiness again."

"Since when do you care about my happiness?" Callie just about hissed at him.

"That's all I've ever cared about," Norman said, trying to control his own anger.

"How about a stroll around town?" Kenny interrupted, trying to ease the tension.

"I think Nellie and I are going to turn in," Norman said, still glaring at his daughter. "You young people go and have a fun time. Don't wander off on your own, Callie."

"I'll make sure we all stay together," Kenny assured him before Callie could say anything else. Norman helped Nellie up, and they made their way out of the restaurant and to their room.

The five young people left the restaurant together and strolled through the town. They looked in all the shop windows, making a mental list of the shops they wanted to come back to for one thing or another.

"Look at all that candy," Eddie said, wide-eyed as he looked through a shop window.

"This is the confectioners," Kenny told him, "would you like to go in and buy something? They're still open."

"I don't have any money," Eddie told him.

Kenny fished around in his pocket and pulled out a silver dollar; which he then handed to his youngest brother. "Go ahead, buy whatever you want," he told him, "it'll be a long time until we see another shop like this."

"Can I get something too?" Michelle asked hopefully.

"You all can," Kenny told her, "Eddie has more than enough to cover whatever you want. Spend it all, and we'll take whatever's left in the wagon with us." Michelle followed Eddie through the door, and Henry followed right behind. When Callie went to follow, Kenny took her by the arm and stopped her.

"What are you doing?" she asked him.

"I won't tell you again," Kenny said to her, "if you ever speak to your parents the way you did in the restaurant, I will spank you until you don't want to sit down for a week."

34

"What do you think gives you the right to do that?" Callie asked.

"Norman is my friend," Kenny said, "I'm not going to watch you make him feel terrible all the time with your unkind words and pouting."

"I'm not pouting," Callie said.

"You are," Kenny said, "I just want you to remember that I've warned you, twice now."

"You wouldn't dare touch me," Callie said, pulling her arm away and quickly walking into the confectioners with the rest of the Johnsons.

"You might be surprised," Kenny muttered as he too followed his family into the shop.

# Chapter 3.  On the Trail

"That should wake everyone," Kenny muttered as he woke to the sound of a bugle echoing through the camp.  He rolled over in his bedroll in the back of the wagon.

"Let's go, Kenny," Henry said from beside him.  "I'm sure Eddie's chomping at the bit to get moving."

"We're going to have to rethink the sleeping arrangements out on the trail.  I don't want Michelle and Eddie sleeping in a wagon alone together.  One of us should be near," Kenny said as he got up and began dressing.

"Maybe we could take turns sleeping under their wagon at night.  I don't know if it's proper for either of us to be in there with Michelle anymore," Henry answered.

"It probably isn't, but we could position their wagon between ours and the Fisher's," Kenny said.  "Callie might even want to sleep with Michelle and Eddie.  Probably be more room than in Norman's wagon."

"We'll have to talk with everyone about that," Henry said.

Before they could say more, Eddie stuck his head in the back of the wagon.  "Come on and get moving," he said excitedly.  "Michelle and Mrs. Fisher are already cooking breakfast; they said we can't leave until we have a good hearty meal."

"You'll need to eat a big breakfast," Kenny told him.  "We'll only stop briefly for a quick lunch before moving out again.  There won't be another hot meal until supper."

"I know.  Mr. Fisher told me," Eddie yelled as he jumped down from the back of their wagon and ran back towards the fire.

"You ready for this?" Kenny asked.

"As ready as I'll ever be," Henry said as he climbed down the back of the wagon, "it's going to be a long hard six months. Sure wish I had Eddie's energy."

"I don't care how long it takes, I just want us to all make it there safe," Kenny told him as he followed him down, "my worst fear is something happening to one of us."

"Don't worry, brother," Henry said, "we'll make it."

"What makes you so sure?" Kenny asked.

"I just feel good about it," Henry answered and shrugged.

"Good morning," Norman said to them both as they joined everyone near the fire.

"Good morning," Henry said, looking around. "Where's Callie?"

"She's pouting in the wagon," Norman told them.

"Why this time?" Kenny asked.

"She talked to her mother in a tone I didn't like last night," Norman told them, "I told her if I heard her do it again; I might just take a hairbrush to her. She's barely spoke to either of us since. I'm enjoying the silence."

"She could use a taste of the hairbrush," Kenny said.

"Problem is, I've never done it before," Norman said. "Callie was always such a good girl. I know she didn't want to leave our home; she's made that clear, but we've been gone from North Carolina for months now. Time to accept it and go back to being the sweet girl she used to be."

"She's always sweet when she's in our wagon," Michelle said as she began filling plates from the pans over the fire. "I know Papa would have taken a hairbrush or strap to me if I didn't talk right to my Mama." She handed Kenny and Henry each a plate.

"Can I have one of those biscuits?" Kenny asked.

37

"Those are for lunch," Michelle told him. "We sliced some ham and fried it already. Once the biscuits cool, we're going to make up sandwiches on them."

"Sounds good," Kenny said, kissing Michelle on the forehead. "Have I told you how happy I am that you decided to come with us?"

"You have," Michelle told him, a big smile on her face, "but I still like hearing it."

"Part of Callie's problem right now is that her Papa's always been too soft on her," Nellie said as she took the pots off of the fire. "One day she's going to need a strong man to bring her back in line."

"I'll be honest," Kenny said, "I threatened to spank her myself if I heard her talk to either of you like she did when we first met."

"I like you, boy," Norman said, "but if you take your hand to my daughter, I'll be finding a preacher, and we'll be having a wedding."

"I'll keep that in mind," Kenny answered as he found a seat and began eating.

Nellie walked over to the Fisher's wagon and called into the back, "if you plan on eating before we leave, you better get out here."

"I'm not hungry," they all heard Callie answer.

"That's your choice," Nellie said to her, "you'll learn. One morning of going hungry isn't going to hurt you."

"There sure are a lot of wagons," Michelle said looking around.

"Harley said at yesterday's meeting we've got sixty-eight wagons and more than three-hundred people traveling together," Kenny told her.

"Is that a lot?" Nellie asked.

"He said about normal," Norman answered.

"What's he like?" Michelle asked.

"Who?" Kenny asked.

"Harley," she said.

"I've only met him briefly at one of the meetings," Kenny told her. "He said he'll be around to get to know everyone better once we get on the trail."

Soon they'd finished eating and reloaded the wagons. Kenny double checked everything to make sure it was tied down well, while Henry hooked up the oxen. Harley Shepard, the wagon master, gave the signal and began heading west, the first wagons on the train fell in right behind him. Henry and Eddie soon joined the line with Kenny and Michelle's wagon following. The Fishers wagon came next.

"Oregon, here we come," the all heard Eddie yell as their journey finally began.

**********

"I don't think I've ever been so tired," Norman said as they sat and ate supper that night.

"How far do you think we went today?" Henry asked.

"I heard Harley say about twelve miles. We did good today," Kenny said.

"Callie," Nellie said to her daughter, "I'd like you to go get some water from the river so we can clean these dishes up; and I don't want to hear any complaining."

Callie nodded but didn't say anything as she grabbed the pail out of the back of the wagon and headed towards the river.

"We really shouldn't let any of the women wander away without one of us," Norman said, going to get up to follow Callie and letting out a groan. "It's probably safe right here, but we should get into the habit of one of us going with them."

"I'll go," Kenny told him, standing up and stretching, "you go ahead and rest up. I need to stretch my legs anyway."

"I'd say it's my daughter and I should be the one to go," Norman said, "but I'm just too doggone tired to move."

"Callie," Kenny called to her, "wait for me."

Callie turned and waited for him to catch up to her, they walked together silently to the river. Callie stood on the bank and looked down both ways. "Sure is quiet out here," she finally said.

"It is," Kenny told her. "I like it."

"I don't mind the quiet," Callie said, "but I don't know if I can do six more months of days like today. It's awful bumpy in the back of the wagon."

"Michelle and Eddie said the same thing about riding on the bench. They're going to see how much of it they can walk tomorrow."

"Maybe I'll walk with them," Callie said. "Might as well walk all the way to Oregon. If I'm lucky I'll fall in a big hole, and the earth will swallow me up."

"Stop talking like that. Can't you just get over it and look forward to something new?" Kenny asked. "Look at it as an adventure."

"I already told you, I never intended to leave North Carolina," Callie answered. "I would have stayed there forever. I tried to talk Mama and Papa into leaving me home, but they wouldn't listen."

"A big part of their decision for this trip is you," Kenny said. "I'm telling you, Callie, war is coming, and you don't want to be anywhere near those states on the east coast when it starts."

"And I'm telling you," Callie said, "you and Papa are making more of this next election than you should. The states may be arguing, but there won't be a war."

"We'll just have to wait and see. So do you want to tell me what happened last night?" Kenny asked.

"Mama and me got into an argument about this trip," Callie told him. "I know you're right, and I need to just get over it because we're on our way, so nothing's going to change."

"What did she say to make you so mad?" Kenny asked.

"Nothing really. Just telling me how glad I'll be once we get there, and how I'll be thanking them for making me come. I'll never thank them for that," Callie said.

"You really feel that way?" Kenny asked.

"I do," Callie said. "Maybe if they would have asked me, or included me in the decision making I'd feel different. But it was just sprung on me one morning." Callie did her best impression of Norman as she continued, "Callie girl, we made a decision, we'll be selling the farm and leaving for Oregon before spring."

Kenny couldn't help but grin at her impression of Norman. "You may not want to hear this," Kenny said, "but I think you should give Oregon a chance. Maybe your Mama is right."

"You're right," Callie said, "I don't want to hear it. At least you and Henry are allowing Michelle to learn to drive the oxen. I'm going to hate walking every day."

"Have you asked Norman to teach you how?" Kenny asked.

"No," Callie admitted, "but he rarely let me drive the buckboard back home. I doubt he'll let me drive this wagon."

"Tomorrow you come over to our wagon after the noon break; I'll teach you how to drive the team," Kenny offered. "We

41

all need to get along on this trip, Callie. You giving grief to your parents makes everyone uncomfortable."

"Well, I'm sorry about that," Callie said, "I'll try to do it when no one is around then."

"I'd prefer you don't do it at all," Kenny said to her.

"Can't make any promises on that," Callie said as she scooped water into the bucket and turned back towards camp. "I do try not to argue, but being cooped up in the back of the wagon with them every night makes it hard."

"I'll take it," Kenny offered, taking the heavy bucket from her. "Henry and I talked this morning; there's room in the back of the wagon Michelle and Eddie are sleeping in if you'd rather sleep there."

"They wouldn't mind?" Callie asked.

"I don't think so," Kenny answered, "plus it'll give your Mama and Papa some privacy. Maybe you won't fight as much."

"I'd like that," Callie said. "I need to get away from them telling me how happy I'm going to be all the time."

"Just try to do better," Kenny said to her. "I meant what I said back near Columbia and in Independence, I'll turn you over my knee if need be."

"Just try it," Callie said, "I'll not allow it."

"Won't matter," Kenny said. "I'd do it anyway."

Callie just looked back at him before she picked up her pace walking back to the wagons.

**********

"Just keep a tight hold on the reins," Kenny said to Callie the next afternoon. "You're doing just fine."

"Thank you for teaching me," Callie said, gripping the reins tighter. "I was surprised Papa agreed to it."

"I've figured out as long as you keep a tight hold, the oxen will follow the wagon in front of them. You just need to watch for the train stopping."

"The oxen won't stop?" Callie asked.

"They haven't so far," Kenny told her, "these animals are stronger than horses, but not as smart."

"I'll remember that," Callie said and smiled, "this isn't so hard."

"Your Papa wants you to be happy," Kenny told her. "He's teaching your Mama how to drive the team on your wagon this afternoon too. If you both know, it'll give him a break sometimes."

"So tell me, Kenny Johnson, what made you decide to go on this journey?" Callie asked, trying to change to subject. "Was it when your parents died?"

"No, I was planning on going with my wife before the accident ever happened," Kenny said. "Henry was going with us."

"You're married?" Callie asked surprised.

"No," Kenny said sadly. "Sadie died in the same wagon accident as my parents. They were taking her home after Sunday supper. Our wedding would have been at the end of February."

"I'm so sorry," Callie told him. "I didn't know."

"It's not something I like to talk about too much," Kenny said.

"One day I'd love to hear about her," Callie said.

"Why?" Kenny asked.

"I believe you're a good man, Kenny," Callie answered. "I'm sure she must have been a lovely woman to have caught your eye and captured your heart."

"She caught my eye when we were just ten-years-old," Kenny admitted. "We went back to school one fall after the harvest, and Sadie and her family had moved into town during the summer."

"Did you notice her right away?" Callie asked.

"Right away," Kenny said and grinned remembering it. "I did everything I could to get her to notice me. I pulled her pigtails, threw mud at her, sent her notes in class. It wasn't until I was sixteen and brought her a bouquet of flowers that she even talked to me."

"You threw mud at her?" Callie asked and laughed. Kenny liked the sound of it.

"I did," he said and began laughing too. "It seemed like a good idea at the time."

"Do you think you'll marry someone else one day?" Callie asked him.

"I don't know what the future holds," Kenny said, surprised at how easy he was finding it to talk to Callie. "I don't know if I'll ever love anyone the way I loved Sadie. But I know I want children, so yes, I'll marry someone else one day."

"I'd like to find a love like that," Callie said to him. "I just don't know if that'll ever happen so far from civilization."

"You do know that the men out west outnumber the women ten to one, don't you?" Kenny asked. "I'm sure there'll be plenty trying to court you."

"That doesn't mean I'll find a good one," Callie said.

"Doesn't mean you won't either," Kenny said. "Tell me about the men you've courted."

"There's only been two," Callie told him. "The first one wanted Papa's farm more than he wanted me."

"How do you know?" Kenny asked.

"When he was around the farm, he barely talked to me," Callie explained. "He just asked about how many acres the farm was, or how many livestock did we have."

"The farm would have been yours when your parents passed?" Kenny asked.

"I'm their only child," Callie answered. "Mama said there were some complications when she had me. They weren't sure if she would survive. After that, she never conceived again."

"What about the second man?" Kenny asked.

"At first I thought he was very sweet," Callie said, "but then one day he got angry and scared me. I told him I didn't want to see him anymore after that."

"Was he angry at you?" Kenny asked.

"No," Callie said, "some children ran out in the road in front of his wagon. I know they were wrong, but the way he screamed at them and threatened them was scary. I knew right then he wasn't for me. I wouldn't want to have children with a man like that."

"You've got a good heart, Callie Fisher," Kenny said to her, "I believe you'll be fighting off the men when we get to Oregon."

"I'll have to get them away from Michelle first," Callie teased and laughed as Kenny frowned.

# Chapter 4.  A Spanking Proposal

"We've had a good week," Harley Shepard, the trail guide, told them as he made his way from fire to fire.  "We're a bit ahead of schedule since the weathers been good, so tomorrow we'll take a day of rest.  The river here should be perfect for washing some clothes if need be."

"Thank goodness," Nellie said softly as she finished her coffee and began preparing their supper, "I'm ready for a day in one place."

"I think we're all ready for a break," Kenny said, "thanks, Harley."

"You people enjoy your rest," Harley said as he moved on to the next fire.

"Did you want me to get the girls up to help you, Nellie?" Henry asked.

"Let them rest," Nellie answered.  "They're both tuckered out after the last week and a half."

"I wonder where we are exactly?" Henry asked.  "I wish I would've bought a map in Independence."

"I bought one; it's in my trunk in the wagon.  I figure we've traveled maybe a hundred-fifty miles so far," Kenny answered.  "We've still got a long way to go."

"I just thought I'd pop in to say hello and introduce myself," a man said as he walked over to where they were gathered around the fire.  "I'm Reverend Drews.  I've been trying to meet a few folks each night after we set up camp."

"Welcome, Reverend," Norman said.  "I'm Norman Fisher, and this is my wife, Nellie.  These young people across from me

46

are Kenny, Henry and Eddie Johnson. We've also got two young women, but they're resting in the back of the wagon at the moment since they walked most of the day. Would you care to join us for a cup of hot coffee?"

"Some other time," the Reverend answered. "I'm just making my rounds and letting everyone know that I'll be conducting a Sunday service tomorrow. I'd be honored if you all attended."

"I think that's a wonderful idea, Reverend Drews," Nellie said. "I pray every day for all of our safety, but a little time to praise the Lord wouldn't hurt either."

"I agree, Nellie," the Reverend said and smiled. They all liked him right away. "I'll wish you all a restful evening."

"Same to you, Reverend," Norman said, "come back when you've got time to sit and visit."

"I most certainly will, and if it's alright with you, I'll bring my wife. God bless you," the Reverend said as Norman nodded at him; he moved on to the next fire.

"What a delightful man," Nellie said.

"Do we really gotta go to church tomorrow, Kenny?" Eddie asked.

"We do," Kenny said, and Henry laughed at the look on Eddie's face. "It won't hurt any of us."

"At least I don't have to take a bath like I used to back home," Eddie said.

"No," Henry said, "but a dip in the river wouldn't hurt you." Eddie got up and laughed as Henry chased him towards the river.

"I've noticed you and Callie spending quite a bit of time together," Norman said to Kenny. "Is there anything I should know about?"

47

"It's not like that," Kenny assured him, "we're friends. When she's not acting like a brat to you and Nellie, I find her easy to talk to."

"I used to find her easy to talk to," Norman admitted, "until we told her we were leaving for Oregon."

"She told me," Kenny said. "I think she's more upset about not being included in the decision to come, than having to come. If that makes sense."

"I just wish she'd let it go and get over her anger," Nellie said. "We've always been so close, but now she barely speaks to me."

"I've warned her about how she speaks to you both," Kenny said. "A good spanking would solve that problem, Norman."

"She'll be twenty in a few days, Kenny," Norman said, "not a young girl that I can turn over my knee anymore. It'll be up to the man she marries to tame her now."

"I've threatened to do it myself more than once," Kenny said.

"I've already told you," Norman said, "if you take your hand to my daughter, I'll be calling the Reverend back."

"That's the only thing that's stopped me," Kenny said to him, and they both grinned.

**\*\*\*\*\*\*\*\*\*\***

"That was a lovely service," Nellie said as the two families walked out of the field where the people from the wagon train had gathered.

"It was," Michelle answered. "I've missed going to church. We haven't been since Mama and Papa died."

"Why not?" Nellie asked.

48

"We were so busy. Kenny had to sell the farm, the livestock still had to be tended, then we had to pack what we were bringing and move Lily's things over to my Grandma and Grandpa's cabin," Michelle explained, "there just wasn't time to make the trip into town."

"Lily is your older sister?" Nellie asked.

"Yes," Michelle said sadly, "she stayed in Kentucky to marry her fiance'. Jeremiah refused to leave and come with us."

"Lucky her," Callie said, glaring at her mother.

"Enough, Callie," Nellie said. "How long are you going to stay mad at us?"

"For the rest of my life," Callie said.

"You sound like a child," Kenny said to her.

"This is none of your business, Kenny Johnson," Callie said as she turned towards him. "Stay out of it."

"You make it everyone's business when you speak like that in front of us," Kenny said to her, taking a deep breath and trying to control his temper.

"Then don't listen," Callie said back, as she too tried to tamper down her anger.

"Now you sound like a brat," Kenny said to her, stepping closer and quieting his voice before adding, "My Papa had a sure-fire remedy for that."

"And what would that be?" Callie asked, looking up at him defiantly.

"A trip to the woodshed or over his knee always seemed to stop that sort of behavior quick enough," Kenny said.

"Stop it, both of you," Michelle tried to say but was ignored by both. "People are beginning to look over at you."

"No one has ever spanked me," Callie said, loud enough for anyone close to hear, "and I'm not going to allow anyone to start now."

"Really?" Kenny asked, his voice surprisingly calm, "and how would you stop me?"

"I'd fight you," Callie said, "and scream."

"You think that would stop me?" Kenny asked, stepping so close that when he looked down at her, they were almost nose-to-nose.

"Remember what I told you, boy," Norman said, "you both need to stop before one of you does something you'll regret."

"You're not man enough to try," Callie said, ignoring Norman and refusing to back down.

"Get the Reverend," Kenny said, picking Callie up and throwing her over his shoulder as he walked towards where his wagon was sitting. "We'll have the wedding as soon as I'm finished."

"Put me down, Kenny. I won't allow you to spank me and I'm not going to marry you," Callie yelled as she hit Kenny in the back.

"I think your Papa may have something to say about that," Kenny said as he landed two firm swats, one on each side of her butt. *Smack, smack.*

"Ouch," Callie yelled, "that hurt."

"You've got more than that coming," Kenny said as he dumped her into the back of his wagon and began climbing up inside himself.

"You stay away from me," Callie said as she tried to get past the crates of supplies at the front of the wagon, so she could crawl out onto the bench and get away. She was beginning to get a bit worried that he was serious.

"You've been asking for this for a long time," Kenny said, as he grabbed her around the waist, carried her over to where a barrel sat; he plopped down on it before flipping Callie over his knee. She began kicking her legs trying to get away. Kenny pulled one of his legs free and placed it on top of hers, firmly holding her in place.

"Let me go!" Callie screamed as loud as she could.

"I think you three should go work on your laundry down by the river," Nellie said outside the wagon to the other three Johnsons.

"I think you're right, Nellie," Henry said as he grabbed the dirty clothes out of the other wagon and headed towards the river, taking his two younger siblings with him.

"What's Kenny doing to Callie?" Eddie asked.

"It's none of our business, Eddie," Nellie heard Michelle say as she walked away.

"I think he's spanking her," Eddie said as he followed Michelle and Henry.

"Do you think I should put a stop to this?" Norman asked his wife. He looked around and saw others watching as they listened to the ruckus going on inside Kenny's wagon.

"Absolutely not," Nellie said, "this spanking has been long overdue. If it gets our sweet, loving daughter to come back, then I'm all for it. Don't you have a preacher to find?"

"I guess I do," Norman said, "I don't think we could have done much better in a son-in-law."

"He's a good one," Nellie said agreeing. "You get going now; I'll stay and make sure things don't get out of hand."

Back in the wagon, Kenny began bringing his hand down on Callie's backside over and over again without saying anything. *Smack, smack, smack, smack, smack, smack, smack, smack, smack,*

*smack, smack, smack, smack, smack, smack, smack, smack, smack, smack, smack.*

"Stop." *Smack, smack.* "That hurts." *Smack, smack.* "Quit." *Smack, smack.* "Wait till my Papa hears about this." *Smack, smack.*

Kenny stopped for a minute, saying, "do you really think your Papa doesn't know what's going on in here?" *Smack, smack, smack, smack, smack, smack, smack, smack, smack, smack, smack, smack, smack, smack, smack, smack, smack, smack, smack.* "Hell, with the ruckus you're making, most of the wagon train probably knows."

"I hope he shoots you," Callie hissed at him.

"He isn't going to shoot me. Husbands are allowed to punish their wives," he told her, beginning again. *Smack, smack, smack, smack, smack, smack, smack, smack, smack, smack, smack, smack, smack, smack, smack, smack, smack, smack, smack.*

"Stop," Callie said, "I'm not your wife, so you have no right to do this."

"You will be by the end of the day," Kenny said right as Callie grabbed his calf and pinched it hard.

"That does it," he said and made a decision. He grabbed the hem of Callie's dress and petticoat and pulled them up to her waist. He wasn't sure if he should be pleased or embarrassed to find her totally bared to him.

"No, Kenny," she said, trying to bring her arm back to pull her skirt down, "you can't do that."

"Really?" he asked as he continued the spanking on her bare bottom. *Smack, smack, smack, smack, smack, smack, smack, smack, smack, smack, smack, smack, smack, smack, smack, smack, smack, smack, smack, smack.* "We need to establish a few things. You let me know when you're ready to be reasonable." *Smack,*

52

*smack, smack, smack, smack, smack, smack, smack, smack, smack, smack, smack, smack, smack, smack, smack, smack, smack, smack, smack.*

"I'm ready," Callie said, crying. The spanking was really starting to hurt, and she didn't know how much more she could take.

"Good," Kenny said, resting his hand on her bottom. "First, you'll treat your parents with respect."

"They didn't..," she started to say, but Kenny raised his hand and started bringing it down again. *Smack, smack, smack, smack, smack, smack.* "I will," she said after a few swats, "I promise."

"Second, you'll come out at night and sit by the fire with everyone else, instead of pouting in the back of the wagon," he continued.

"What if I don't want.." she again started to argue but was cut off. *Smack, smack, smack, smack, smack, smack.* "I'll come out by the fire," she quickly said.

"And you'll join in the conversation," Kenny said.

"What if I don't.." she started to protest again. *Smack, smack, smack, smack, smack, smack.* "I'll join in."

"And you'll be the kind, funny, intelligent woman that I like to spend time with," Kenny added.

"I'll try," Callie said. *Smack, smack, smack, smack, smack, smack.*

"You'll succeed," Kenny said.

"I will," Callie said, wanting the spanking to end.

Kenny leaned over, opened one of the trunks and grabbed his mama's hairbrush out of the side pocket where he'd seen Michelle place it. He then pulled Callie up tighter against him. He knew she really wasn't going to like what happened next.

53

"No more, Kenny," Callie said, "please, I've had enough."

"Not yet," Kenny told her and brought the brush down twice on each already red butt cheek. *Splat, splat, splat, splat.*

"Ouch," Callie yelled each time. "Ouch, ouch, ouch."

"Now let's talk about our marriage," Kenny said to her.

"I don't want to marry you," Callie said.

"Everyone knows what I brought you into this wagon for," Kenny told her. "We have to marry."

"But you don't love me," Callie said to him, "you said yourself, you don't think you'll ever love anyone like you did Sadie."

"But I like you," Kenny said, "I like you a lot."

"I won't do it," Callie said.

"We can have a good marriage, Callie," Kenny said, bringing the brush down again, but this time on her thighs. *Splat, splat, splat, splat.* "I'll treat you with respect as long as you treat me the same way." *Splat, splat, splat, splat.*

"But I want to marry a man I love," Callie said, then added, "and loves me."

"Maybe we'll learn to love each other," Kenny told her, pulling her skirt down and flipping her over to sit on his lap.

"Let me up, Kenny," Callie said, trying to jump off his lap, but he was holding her too tightly. "It hurts to sit."

"Not yet," Kenny said, wrapping his arms more firmly around her. "Not until you agree to marry me."

"Is that what you really want?" Callie asked.

"I always knew I'd marry," Kenny said. "I do want a family, Callie, don't you?"

"Someday," Callie said sadly, "but I wanted to raise them with someone who respects and loves me, not someone I had to marry because they spanked me."

54

"Say you'll marry me, Callie," Kenny said quietly, "and I'll show you more respect than you've ever been given before, and maybe love will come later."

"I don't want you to spank me again," Callie said to him, her face turning red.

"That I can't promise," Kenny told her, he reached up and gently wiped the tears from her cheeks. "You're getting spanked or not depends on you."

"What do you mean?" Callie asked.

"Act like the kind young woman I know you can be, and you'll have nothing to worry about," Kenny told her. "Just do as I say and don't put yourself in danger. That's all I ask."

"What if I don't agree with you?" Callie asked.

"Then you talk to me, and we'll see if a compromise can be reached," Kenny told her.

Callie thought about it for a long while. She knew there wasn't much she could do to get out of the wedding. The two of them had been in the wagon for much too long alone, plus she knew he was right, most of the camp probably knew what was happening.

"I'll marry you," she barely whispered. "I have no choice. But know that if this doesn't work, I'll be leaving and going back to North Carolina."

"How would you get back there?" Kenny asked her, not wanting to let her off his lap.

"I'd always planned on going back," she said. "I just hadn't figured out how to get there yet."

"You won't be going back," Kenny said.

"We'll see," Callie whispered.

\*\*\*\*\*\*\*\*\*

55

Kenny led Callie to the back of the wagon and helped her climb down. He looked out and seen not just Nellie and Norman, but Reverend Drews and Harley.

"I hear we're going to have a wedding, son," Reverend Drews said smiling.

"Yes, sir," Kenny answered, "as soon as my bride is ready." Callie just stared at the ground.

"Come," Nellie said, taking her gently by the arm, "let's find you a dress and wash your face a bit first." Callie didn't say anything but let Nellie lead her away.

"I'll be out shortly," Kenny said and started to go back into the wagon when Harley spoke up.

"I don't need to get my shotgun, do I?" Harley asked, only half joking.

"Nope," Kenny answered, "I'm more than willing to marry Callie."

He went back into the wagon and again opened the trunk where they'd packed many of his Mama's prized possessions. He put the brush back into the side pocket before beginning his search. He moved the clothes and items around until he reached the bottom and found the small pouch he'd been looking for. Inside were his Mama and Papa's wedding bands. Eddie and Lily wanted the bury their parents wearing them, but the Reverend at the church talked them out of it. He was glad that he'd taken them now. He put them in his pocket and grabbed a clean shirt, britches, and a cloth for washing before jumping out of the back of the wagon and heading for the river. He too could use a quick wash.

"Hey, brother," Henry greeted him. He'd helped Michelle finished the laundry, and it was spread out on the river bank to dry in the sun. Eddie was splashing around swimming while they watched.

"You been here long?" Kenny asked.

"Just since you took Callie into the wagon," Henry said. "How did that go?"

"Better than I expected. How long until all these clothes are dry?" Kenny asked.

"With the sun, not long. Why?" Henry said.

"Because I'll be getting married soon," Kenny told him. "I'd like you all to be back at the wagon to attend."

"Callie?" Henry asked.

"Who else?" Kenny said.

"You sure about this?" Henry asked. "She's a nice enough girl, but I don't like the way she treats Norman and Nellie."

"I think you'll be seeing a change in her," Kenny said as he began washing himself off best he could.

"Do you love her?" Michelle asked him.

"Not yet," he told her, "but I do like her a lot."

"We all like her, but is that good enough to marry?" Michelle asked.

"It's going to have to be," Kenny said. "I still love Sadie, but with time, who knows what'll happen. It'll all work out."

"I hope so," Henry said to him as he and Michelle started collecting the clothes that were already dry.

"So do I," Kenny said quietly, so no one else could hear.

# Chapter 5. A Trail Wedding

"Do you have rings?" the Reverend asked Kenny quietly after Callie said her 'I will'. "I can skip that part if need be."

"I've got rings," Kenny said, digging down into his pocket and pulling them out, surprising Callie.

"They're beautiful," she said, looking at the rings in his hand.

"They were my Mama and Papa's," Kenny told her; she nodded and glanced up and looked at him for the first time since the ceremony began, but quickly looked back at the ground.

"I'll take good care of it," she told him.

"Place the ring on her finger and repeat after me," the Reverend said. "I, Kenneth John Johnson, take thee, Callie Marie Fisher, to be my wedded wife."

"I, Kenneth John Johnson, take thee, Callie Marie Fisher, to be my wedded wife," Kenny repeated.

"To have and to hold, from this day forward," the Reverend said.

"To have and to hold, from this day forward," Kenny repeated.

"For better, for worse, for richer, for poorer, in sickness and in health, to love, and to cherish, till death us do part," the Reverend continued.

Again Kenny repeated, "for better, for worse, for richer, for poorer, in sickness and in health, to love, and to cherish, till death us do part."

"According to God's holy ordinance: and thereto I give thee my faith," the Reverend concluded.

"According to God's holy ordinance: and thereto I give thee my faith," Kenny finished.

"Now you," the Reverend said to Callie and repeated the words with her. The difference was that when she spoke, it was so softly no one except Kenny and the Reverend could hear her.

"I now pronounce you man and wife," the Reverend said. He then looked out at everyone that came to witness the wedding, which was almost everyone on the wagon train. He smiled at them and said, "this is my favorite part. You may now kiss your bride."

Kenny gently cupped Callie's chin in his hand and lifted her head until she was looking right at him. Her face was bright red. He leaned down and gently pressed his lips to hers, sealing the marriage.

Callie's stomach fluttered, and she was surprised at how much she enjoyed the kiss. When Kenny pulled back, he stood silently looking right into her eyes while everyone watching began to clap and cheer.

"Everyone," Nellie said loudly, "I know words got around that there's going to be a grand meal tonight. Harley has said those with fiddles should get them out. We'll eat, dance and celebrate."

"You up for a little dancing, Mrs. Johnson?" Kenny asked her.

"You dance?" Callie asked.

"Of course," Kenny said. "Don't you want to?"

"I'd love to dance, Mr. Johnson," Callie said nervously, as she took his hand and they led everyone to where the buffet had been set up.

Kenny couldn't believe the amount of food that'd been prepared. Every wagon must've pitched in and cooked something. There were beans with bacon, and beans with salt pork. There were more than a few different types of rice, some with meat and some without.  There was potato salad, and some jars of fruit. Someone had even made a big pot of beef stew with some jerky they must have been carrying.  At the end of the makeshift table, there were all different kinds of bread and pies, with homemade jams and jellies.  Nellie even went through the trouble of whipping up a chocolate cake, Callie's favorite.

"I'll be right back," Kenny said, dropping her off at the food.  "I want to check on Michelle and Eddie."  She just nodded at him.

"There's so much," Callie said as she filled the plate her Mama handed her.

"People need something to celebrate once in a while," Nellie told her.  "It brings out the good in people."

"I just wish everyone didn't need to know why we had to get married," Callie said quietly to her Mama.

"What do they know?" Nellie asked.  "You and Kenny have been spending time together almost every day since we met. He's even taught you how to drive his team.  They all thought you were courting anyway."

"We're just friends, Mama," Callie said.  "He's still in love with his fiance', Sadie.  He'll never love me."

"She's not his fiance' anymore, Callie, you're his wife.  He loves you," Nellie told her, "you just wait and see.  Your Papa and I both noticed a week ago how he watches you.  He just hasn't realized it yet."

"You think so, Mama?" Callie asked.

"I know so," Nellie said.  "How do you feel about him?"

"He's become my best friend," Callie said.  "I don't know if I feel anything more than that."

"You do," Nellie said, "when he's not watching you, you're watching him."

"I do not," Callie protested but smiled slightly. Nellie was glad to see her sweet daughter returning.

"You do," Nellie said, and then laughed as Callie blushed.

**********

"I'd like you all to meet my wife, Julia," Reverend Drews said as he joined them with an obviously pregnant woman. "Julia, these are the Fishers and Johnsons."

"It's lovely to meet all of you," Julia Drews said.

"You too, dear," Nellie answered. "When is your baby due?"

"Most likely before we get to Oregon," Julia said. "Hopefully, we'll be at a fort; I'm worried about giving birth on the trail."

"I've already found a doctor traveling with us, just in case," Reverend Drews assured her.

"Where do you plan on settling?" Norman asked the couple.

"A small town called McMinnville, it's in the Willamette Valley," the Reverend answered. "You ever hear of it?"

"I saw it on a map and I've already bought land around there," Kenny told him.

"We'll be looking for something in that area too so that we can stay close to our daughter," Norman said.

"Nothing like a trail wedding," Harley said as he joined them. "There's always a couple on every train I've led."

"It was a fun day," Michelle answered. "How many times have you made this trip, Mr. Shepard?"

"Just call me Harley, young lady," he answered. "This is my eighth and final trip to Oregon."

"You're not going back?" Henry asked.

"Not this time," Harley explained. "My brother, Roland, and myself bought a good chunk of land out there last year. This year we'll stay and start homesteading it."

"Your brothers in the train?" Kenny asked.

"No," Harley said. "He'll be meeting me there. He's the trail boss for another train leaving out of Independence in mid-May."

"My friend Nick will be coming out about that time. I wonder if he'll be traveling with your brother?" Kenny said.

"There's a good chance he will," Harley told them. "The last trains will leave by the end of May, anything later than that and you may not make it across the Rockies."

"Where's your land at?" Henry asked.

"You ever hear of the Willamette Valley?" Harley asked.

"Hey that's where we're going," Eddie chimed in with his mouthful of pie. Kenny was going to scold him and then decided to let it go this time. Eddie looked happy again, and that's all Kenny really cared about.

"It'll be good to know some folks in the area," Harley said.

"One more dance before we turn in?" Kenny asked as he held out his hand to Callie.

"Yes," she said and put her hand in his. She hadn't had this much fun or danced so much in a long time. Kenny helped pull her up off the stool she'd been sitting on and took her out with the other couples where he spun her around.

"You've been very quiet today," Kenny said to her.

"I'm embarrassed," she said.

"Why?" Kenny asked.

"Everyone knows what happened in the wagon, and why we married," she answered.

"Who cares," Kenny said and shrugged, "it's none of their business. There are bigger things to worry about on this trip, in a week no one will remember why we married."

"Do you really believe that?" Callie asked, and Kenny nodded.

"Did you have a good time today?" Kenny asked.

"Most of it," Callie teased, "the part right after church wasn't so good."

"Ah," Kenny said and grinned, "the spanking. Are you still sore?"

"Only when I sit down," Callie said to him. "I can't wait to lie down."

"We can go to our wagon whenever you want," Kenny said and then seen her smile turn into a frown and felt her stiffen. "What's wrong?"

"I'm not ready," Callie started to say.

"Shh," Kenny said to her. "Let's say our goodnights and then walk a bit. I was planning on talking to you about tonight, but not here."

"Alright," Callie said, and she let him lead her around as they thanked everyone and said their farewells.

"I didn't think we'd ever get out of there, I think we met just about everyone traveling with us today," Kenny said as he finally led her down to the river. "Did I tell you how beautiful you looked today?"

"I did not," Callie said, once again blushing.

"You did," Kenny said, sitting down on the grass and patting the spot next to him. "Come sit beside me."

"I'll kneel," She said, not wanting to put any pressure on her still tender cheeks.

"How's this?" Kenny asked as he pulled her down to sit on his lap. "Should be softer than the ground."

"It is," Callie said, her blush getting brighter. "What did you want to talk about?"

"Tonight," he began. When Callie said nothing he continued, "I know this marriage happened fast. I want to give you time to get to know me as more than your friend and become comfortable with me as your husband. Until you say you're ready, nothing will happen between us."

"Nothing?" Callie said, not sure if she was happy or a bit disappointed.

"I think a kiss every now and then would be all right," Kenny said.

"Just a kiss?" she asked. She actually enjoyed the kiss he'd given her at the end of the wedding ceremony. She was curious to see if she'd like it again.

"More than one, but that's a good start," he said to her and again used his hand to cup her face and turn it to his.

Kenny pressed his lips to hers and then waited patiently until she began to kiss him back. Not wanting to go too far, he broke the first kiss and then gave her two more.

"That's enough," he said to her.

"Why?" she asked. "Did I do something wrong?"

"What did your Mama tell you about your wedding night?" Kenny asked.

"That's too embarrassing to tell you," Callie said, smiling shyly.

"Tell me," Kenny teased. "They're your Mama's words, not yours."

"She just said to let you lead. She said you'd be taking your rod and putting it in my sheath. That it might hurt the first time, but it would get better each time after," Callie said, looking everywhere but at him. "I think I know what she means, but I'm not sure."

"Callie you do know that a man has a cock and a woman has an entrance for it, right?" Kenny asked.

"Of course," Callie said, "I did grow up on a farm, I've seen the pigs, horses and cows breed."

"Well," Kenny said, taking her hand. "Just like with farm animals, when a man is attracted to a woman, his cock will grow." he placed her hand on top of this pants where his cock was. It was rock hard. "I'm trying to be a gentleman and get to know you, but if we keep kissing, I'll be taking your virginity tonight."

"Oh," Callie said and quickly pulled her hand away as Kenny lifted her off his lap

"Have you ever done it before?" Callie asked him. She was glad it was dark so Kenny couldn't see her face become even redder.

"Only a few times," Kenny answered.

"With Sadie?" Callie asked.

"No," Kenny answered quickly. "Sadie and I both agreed to wait until we were married, but I'll be honest, we did other things."

"Like what?" Callie asked.

"We kissed a lot," Kenny told her, "and touched each other."

"Touched each other?" Callie asked.

"You don't need to have relations with someone to give them pleasure," Kenny explained. It was his turn to be glad it was dark, he knew his own cheeks were now red. "You can use your hand or mouth to touch each other. I can't explain it, Callie, but when you're ready, I'll show you."

"Alright," Callie said, "I'll tell you when I'm ready. So what do we do now?" Callie asked.

"We go back to the wagon," he told her. "Just because I want to give you time before we consummate this marriage, doesn't mean we won't be sleeping together at night."

"In the same wagon?" she asked.

"In the same wagon, and the same bed," Kenny said to her. "You ready?" He got up and again offered her his hand, which she tentatively took, and he led her to the wagon that was now considered theirs.

# Chapter 6.  Becoming More than Friends

"Tell me about them," Callie said to Kenny, smiling at him as she rode in the wagon with him a few days later.  She'd spent the morning walking behind the wagons with Michelle and Eddie, but Kenny asked her to ride with him after lunch.

"You'd love them, and Grandma would love you," Kenny said to her.  "I think Grandma really wanted to come out here with us, but she knew she'd never get Grandpa to agree."

"Why?" Callie asked.  "Was he afraid the trip would be too hard on them?  I'm amazed at some of the older people I've seen with us."

"They could make it.  Grandma and Grandpa may be older, but they're both strong and in good health.  Grandma's family moved around pretty often when she was younger, but Grandpa's lived in Kentucky almost his whole life.  It's not like we're the only grandkids they have.  My Papa had two brothers and a sister.  We've got fifteen cousins from them alone," Kenny explained.

"Do they all still live in Paducah?" Callie asked.

"Not all of them.  Two of my Aunts moved to the next town after they married, all their children live at home, but everyone else is either in the town or on a farm nearby," Kenny told her.

"And you didn't want to stay near them?" Callie asked.

"Not if I was going to be forced into fighting in a war I don't see anyone winning," Kenny said to her.

"You really think there's going to be a war, don't you?" Callie said, making it into more of a comment than a question.

"I do," Kenny said. "I don't want to see my cousins fighting against each other, but it's going to happen."

"Some of them would fight for the north?" Callie asked.

"Probably half of them," Kenny said. "No one in North Carolina would?"

"Not that I ever heard," Callie said. "Most support slavery, but Papa and Mama never did."

"My parents either," Kenny said. "My Uncle Joe has a couple though."

"Slaves?" Callie asked.

"Yep," Kenny said, "we never went to their home to visit. My Mama refused, we only saw those cousins when my Aunt Maisie would come home to visit Grandma and Grandpa."

"We know quite a few people with slaves," Callie said.

They both became silent as they rode on, thinking about home. Neither one was uncomfortable with the silence. They'd been married for almost a week, and Kenny had been keeping his word. Every evening when they crawled into the back of the wagon, he kissed her goodnight and then pulled her against him with his arm around her. But he didn't try anything more until the sound of the bugle woke them in the morning, then he'd always steal another kiss. The last couple of days he'd made the kisses last just a tad bit longer. This morning he'd even used his tongue.

"We should be stopping for the night soon," Callie said.

"We should," he agreed. "Maybe tonight after supper you'd like to take a stroll around the area with me?"

"I'd love too," Callie said and smiled at him. It was a smile Kenny looked forward to seeing more and more every day.

\*\*\*\*\*\*\*\*\*\*

"I thought I'd come check on the newlyweds," Reverend Drews said as he found them on the edge of a small grove of trees

68

collecting firewood. "What's it been? Two weeks since you married?"

"That sounds about right," Kenny answered, "but each day out here seems like three doesn't it?"

"Howdy, Reverend," Callie said. "How's Julia feeling?"

"She's doing well, but I worry about her and the baby all the time," Reverend Drews answered. "I'll be just as glad as everyone else to get to Oregon and settle."

"I'm surprised you didn't wait another year before making the trip," Kenny said to him.

"I suggested it," Reverend Drews told them, "but Julia knew when I married her I was planning to come west. She said she'd rather make the trip this year while she carried our baby, then wait until next year when she'd have a baby to care for and possibly another on the way."

"This is a hard trip, much harder than I expected," Kenny admitted, "but I hear now that we're out on the plains we won't have as many hills to go over."

"But the storms can be fierce," Reverend Drews said. "I'm counting on the Lord to keep us all safe."

"Us too Reverend," Callie said, smiling. "Maybe you and Julia would like to join us for supper one day this week?"

"We'd love to do that," Reverend Drews said to her. "I've been trying to get to know everyone on the train, but it takes time."

"You should have time, we've got a long way to go yet," Kenny said.

"That we do," the Reverend answered. "Can I give you a hand with that kindling?"

"Sure, Reverend," Kenny answered. "I hear soon we won't be able to find wood and we'll be using buffalo chips."

"What are those?" Callie asked.

"Buffalo poop," Kenny answered, and both he and Reverend Drews laughed at the look of horror on her face.

**********

"I don't think I'm ever going to get this mud out of Henry's britches," Callie said as she scrubbed some of their laundry down by the river where they were camped. Harley was giving them another day of rest since they were a few days ahead of schedule.

Reverend Drews had conducted Sunday service again that morning. Now everyone was off doing different things. Some of the women were sewing, baking, or doing laundry, while the men fixed wagons, checked yokes and leather straps, or tended to their livestock. Once they were done, they either socialized with others or rested around their wagons. It had put a smile on just about everyone's face as they all watched the children run around and play.

"Those were the ones he had on the other day when it rained so hard," Kenny said, "we were both in mud up to our knees trying to lead the oxen. I should have a pair just as bad," he leaned over to look at what she was doing, and Callie took her hand and splashed him in the face with the water.

"Why did you do that?" Kenny said as he wiped his face and looked down at her, Callie was looking up at him holding back her laughter.

"I was just playing around, Kenny," Callie said as she stood up.

"You wanna play?" Kenny asked. "Maybe you need a dip in the river."

"No, Kenny," Callie said laughing. Kenny lunged for her, but Callie took off running. They were both laughing hard as they ran past the wagon where her Mama and Papa were resting outside. Nellie just shook her head and smiled as they ran past.

70

"What's Kenny doing to Callie?" Eddie asked as he looked up from the stick Norman was teaching him to carve.

"They're just playing," Norman said, he too smiled. The difference in his daughter since she'd married Kenny had been something to see. She seemed almost happy again.

Callie ran as fast as she could, but she was laughing so hard her side was beginning to hurt. She swung back down towards the river with Kenny right behind her.

"Got you," he said as she finally had to slow and he grabbed hold of her and swung her up into his arms.

Kenny carried her back to the river and walked a couple of feet out into it before he stopped. "Maybe you need a bath," he said and pretended he was going to drop her.

"No," Callie squealed and threw her arms around his neck. "Don't do it, Kenny," Kenny walked out just a little deeper into the water.

"Do what?" Kenny said and pretended to drop her again.

"Kenny," she squealed again and tightened her grip around his neck, pulling her body in tight to his.

"It'll cost you," Kenny said again, letting her go for a split second.

"Whatever you want," Callie said, "just don't let go."

"A kiss," Kenny said and pressed his lips to hers. He let his tongue touch her lips, and she parted them and sucked it into her mouth, letting it tangle with her own.

"Little lady," Harley said from the bank, "I was coming to see what all that screaming was about, but it looks like you're in good hands to me."

Callie broke the kiss, and her face turned red as she turned to look at Harley. "We were just playing around," she said to him.

71

"So I see," Harley said, "carry on." He walked away smiling and shaking his head.

"I need to finish washing our clothes," Callie said to Kenny, embarrassed now that they'd been interrupted.

"I'll take you back to shore," Kenny told her, a bit disappointed, but he swooped in for one last kiss as he carried her there.

**********

Kenny dove under the cold water as he tried to get himself together. He didn't know how much longer he could stand it. He'd been married to Callie for more than three weeks, and still, she hadn't given him any sign that she was ready to make their marriage real. Each night for the last week when they crawled into the wagon and got into their makeshift bed, he'd pull her over into his arms. Each morning when he woke his cock would be rock hard, and he'd sneak out of the wagon as quietly as he could to take a dip in whatever river or lake they were near.

He was going to have to make a move soon. This morning when he woke, he'd been cupping her breast, the size fit perfectly into his hand. He'd laid there for a few minutes longer not wanting to let go.

"Good morning, brother," Henry said as he made his way down to the river. "Your wife and mother-in-law sent me to tell you breakfast will be ready in just a few minutes."

"I'm coming," Kenny told him as he made his way out of the river and began to dress in clean, dry clothes.

"You and Callie doing alright?" Henry asked.

"Of course we are," Kenny said, "why do you ask?"

"You seem to spend a lot of mornings swimming down at the river if there's one near camp," Henry said.

"We're fine," Kenny said. "How are you and the others holding up?"

"We'll make it," Henry said. "Eddie's getting quite good at driving the team. I think he's grown two inches and put on a good ten pounds since we left Paducah."

"I've noticed that," Kenny said, "hope he doesn't outgrow all his clothes before we get to Oregon."

Henry laughed, "we may have to purchase some things at one of the forts. I'm glad Mama taught Michelle how to sew."

"Me too," Kenny said and clapped him on the back as they made their way back to camp. "I think I remember Michelle buying some material in Independence. We'll have to ask her about that."

They talked all the way back to the fire where his wife was helping the rest of the women cook, Kenny stopped and took a plate from her and said, "thank you."

"It's your favorite this morning," Callie told him, "flapjacks and bacon."

"How did you know that was my favorite?" Kenny asked.

"You always eat twice as much when we have it," Callie said to him smiling. "I just put on a second helping for you."

"I do love me some flapjacks," Kenny admitted. He didn't know what came over him, but he leaned forward and kissed Callie in front of everyone. Something he'd never done before. Michelle blushed and smiled, glad Kenny seemed happy again.

"Yuck," Eddie said, making everyone laugh.

"You won't think it's yuck in a few years, squirt," Henry said to him, giving his hair the customary ruffle.

"Would you like to ride with me today, Callie?" Nellie asked.

"Where's Papa going to be?" Callie asked.

"He's going to ride out with the scouts this morning," Nellie said. "They said we might see some buffalo today; Papa's going with some of the other men to hunt. You know what a good hunter he is, he can't wait to get one of those buffalo."

"If Kenny doesn't need me to drive our wagon, I'd love to ride with you, Mama," Callie said.

"Michelle can drive our team for a bit this afternoon if Norman isn't back yet," Kenny assured her. "You and your Mama enjoy some time together today."

"Alright," Callie said, giving Kenny one of her big smiles, she'd been hoping for a chance to talk to Nellie in private anyway.

Once everyone had eaten, they quickly packed up the wagons. Michelle and Kenny climbed into one, Henry and Eddie into another, and as Norman rode off with the scouts, Callie joined Nellie on the bench of the Fisher's wagon.

"So how are you and Kenny getting along?" Nellie asked as she steered their oxen and wagon into the line and began moving forward.

"So far we've gotten along well," Callie said.

"I thought so," Nellie said and smiled at her daughter. "I do believe that young man loves you."

"You're wrong, Mama," Callie said sadly. "He'll always be in love with Sadie, he's told me so."

"He'll always hold a place for her in his heart, Callie," Nellie said, "but he can still love you too."

"He doesn't," Callie said. "I have to settle for being friends."

"The secret to a man's feelings comes at night when you're alone," Nellie told her and Callie blushed.

"Why are you blushing so?" Nellie asked. "You're a married woman now; you know what I'm talking about."

"I don't, Mama," Callie reluctantly told her. "Kenny said he'd wait until we knew each other and I was ready. He's never done more than kiss me."

"And what do you feel when he kisses you?" Nellie asked.

"I like it," Callie again admitted.

"Are you ready for more?" Nellie asked.

"I think so," Callie said to her.

"Have you told your young man that?" Nellie asked.

"No," Callie said, "but I haven't stopped him from trying more either."

"He's waiting for you, Callie," Nellie said seriously. "Talk with him, tell him how you feel. He's a good man; even your Papa likes him."

"Do you really think I should?" Callie asked.

"Absolutely," Nellie answered.

\*\*\*\*\*\*\*\*\*\*

"I'm glad you're back riding with me," Kenny told Callie as they resumed their way west after their midday break.

"Are you?" Callie asked.

"Of course I am," Kenny said, glancing over at her. "Is something wrong?"

"Not really," Callie said.

"Talk to me, Callie," Kenny said to her. "I can tell something is bothering you."

"Nothing is bothering me," Callie said nervously.

"Something is," Kenny said. "You're my wife; you can tell me anything."

"I'm not really your wife," Callie said softly.

"What do you mean?" Kenny asked her. "Please, talk to me, Callie."

75

"Do you think you'll ever be able to love me? Even a little bit? Or will Sadie always come between us?" Callie fired off questions.

"First, Sadie is not between us," Kenny said to her. "I loved her, but she's gone now. I truly believe she'd want me to move on. Second, I hope that one day we can learn to love each other. What brought this up?"

"I just," Callie began and then quit talking.

"Tell me," Kenny said, glancing over at her quickly before turning his eyes back on the wagon in front of him.

"I want to be your wife," she said softly.

"In every way?" Kenny asked hopefully.

"Yes," she said quietly again. "But I don't want to find that we don't suit afterword. I know we're friends, but I want to be more than that."

"We'll suit," Kenny said confidently. Although she wasn't Sadie, Kenny found that every day he liked Callie more. She was hardworking, rarely complained anymore, and was always willing to pitch in to do her share. Kenny thought hard for a minute and realized; he hadn't really thought about Sadie in days, his thoughts were now filled with Callie most of the time. "You and I were friends, Callie, but don't you think we've become more than that the last few weeks? I look forward to getting back to you when we're apart; I can't wait to see you smile every morning, I think you're smart, kind and beautiful. I can't say that I love you yet, because I'm not sure how I feel. I know that I want to kiss you every time I see you, and I love that you've made me want to live again. I'm making a mess of my words."

"I think you're doing pretty well," Callie said.

"What I'm trying to get to, is that nothing would make me happier than to make you my wife, fully," Kenny said to her.

"Tonight?" Callie asked and glanced up at him. Although her face was very red, she smiled at him.

"Tonight," Kenny said to her. "This day is going to last forever." He then leaned over and kissed her soundly on the lips, deep and long, not caring who saw them.

# Chapter 7. Finally

"That was a fine meal, ladies," Kenny said as he sat at the makeshift table and drank a cup of coffee.

"I'm glad you enjoyed it," Nellie said to him. "Do you think Harley will give us the day off of traveling Sunday? The fresh meat from the buffalo you men killed today tasted so good, but it won't last more than a few days with this heat. Be nice if you had time to hunt for more."

"There was enough meat on that buffalo to give every wagon enough for a meal or two," Norman said. "Too bad we can't stop for a few days, then we'd have time to make some jerky."

"We're making good time," Kenny answered. "We should pass Chimney Rock tomorrow."

"Then what's next?" Eddie asked as he yawned.

"We should get to Fort Laramie in a couple of weeks. Harley said if we keep ahead of schedule like this, we'll be able to spend a few days there. The animals can rest, we'll see what supplies we're low on and restock, and maybe we'll even get a dance in," Henry told him. "If you're tired, why don't you turn in, squirt?"

"I was waiting for you," Eddie said to him, "or Michelle."

"I've got guard duty tonight, remember?" Henry reminded his little brother. "That's why we made sure you and Michelle's wagon was between the Fisher's and Kenny's."

"I hate when you have guard duty," Michelle said, "I always feel safer when you're under the wagon at night."

"Don't worry, Michelle," Norman said to her, "if you hear or see anything during the night that even makes you a little nervous or scared, just call out. Kenny and I'll come running."

"I'll keep you safe, Michelle," Eddie said as he once again yawned, "don't worry." Everyone smiled, not wanting to hurt Eddie's feeling by laughing.

"I have no doubt you would try, squirt," Henry said, ruffling his hair. "Come on; I'll walk you the wagon so you can get settled before I have to leave." He turned to Michelle and added, "I'll only be on guard duty for a few hours, so I'll be sleeping under the wagon before you know it."

"Good," Michelle said and Henry gave her a quick hug.

"Henry," they heard Eddie ask as he walked away with Henry, "why do you always call me squirt?"

"I guess I always have," they heard Henry answer, "but if you keep growing, I'll have to stop soon, you're almost as tall as Kenny and me."

"What about you, Kenny?" Norman asked. "No guard duty tonight?"

"No," Kenny said, glancing at his wife, "but I do think Callie and I are going to turn in early, it's been a tiring day."

"You two run along," Nellie said to them, winking at her daughter, "Michelle and I'll finish up the dishes. I'll have Norman walk Michelle to the wagon after."

"You sure you don't mind, Mama?" Callie asked nervously. "I can help if you need me. I don't want to leave you and Michelle with extra work."

"It's only a few dishes," Michelle said, "if you're both tired, go turn in. I don't mind staying and helping. I'm not tired enough to sleep yet anyway."

79

"Thank you, little sister," Kenny said, walking over and kissing her on the forehead. Telling her again, "I'm so glad you decided to come with us. I sure would have missed you."

"I miss Lily, and Grandma and Grandpa," Michelle said sadly. "Do you think they're alright?"

"I gave them our destination in Oregon," Kenny assured her. "I'm sure by the time we arrive there'll be a bunch of letters from all of them."

"How can that be?" Michelle asked.

"The mail runs faster than these wagon trains do. I heard you can get a letter all the way from Oregon to anywhere on the east coast in less than a month," Kenny explained.

"I hope you're right," Michelle said.

"I've heard the same," Norman said. "I bet there'll be a stack of letters by the time we get to Oregon just waiting for you."

Michelle didn't say anything else; she began stacking the dishes in the pot of hot water she'd just pulled away from the fire. She really did hope they were right. She watched as Kenny walked over and extended his hand to Callie, helping her up from the stool she'd been sitting on.

"Good night, Mama. Good night, Papa," Callie said as she stood and took Kenny's arm; he led her towards the wagon where their bedding had already been laid out.

"Sleep well, daughter," Nellie said, trying to hide her smile as they walked away.

Kenny helped Callie climb in the back of the wagon and made sure that the cover was tied securely so no one could see inside. When he turned back to Callie, she was looking at him nervously.

"I need to put my nightgown on," she said quietly. She was surprised when Kenny climbed in after her, thinking he was going to do the same thing he'd been doing for the last three weeks; wait outside while she changed.

"You don't need one tonight," he said as he reached over and pulled her into his arms. "I know you're nervous, Callie. We'll take it as slow as you need too."

"I am nervous," Callie admitted, "but I think I'm excited too."

"Good to know," Kenny said right before he kissed her.

He started gently, pressing his lips to hers repeatedly before finally sealing his lips over hers and sliding his tongue into her mouth until it touched her own, and letting them tangle together. He ran his hands gently up and down her back, not letting her body away from his. Kenny felt his cock harden instantly.

He backed up a step so he could sit on one of the trunks, taking her with him. He stood her between his knees and turned her around. He began unbuttoning her dress slowly, running his hands over her back occasionally as he went along. Once he had the last button undone, he turned her back towards him. Callie didn't say anything but looked at his face as he reached up and peeled the dress off of her, exposing her breasts to him for the first time. He let her dress pool at her feet as she stood in front of him in just a single petticoat. Once again he noticed her face begin to get red.

When Kenny pulled her dress off Callie's first thought was to bring her hands up and cover herself, but the look on Kenny's face made her want to see what happened next. She felt her cheeks grow warm as he dropped his eyes down to stare at her chest. She felt his hands slide up her sides, loving the feel of them on her bare skin. His hands slid around to her back and he pulled her forward, licking over one of her nipples before pulling it into his mouth and sucking on it gently. His other hand came up and cupped the other breast; he began running his thumb back and forth across the nipple. With him sucking on one and playing with the other, Callie felt them both harden and let out a small moan.

Kenny let his mouth and fingers play with her breasts for just a minute longer before he pulled back from her. He unbuttoned his own shirt and peeled it off his shoulders, exposing his chest to her. Callie reached out and tentatively touched him. He put his hand over hers, holding it above his heart.

"I can feel your heart beating," she said quietly, and grinned, "are you nervous too?"

"Nervous, excited, a bit scared," Kenny admitted.

"Why are you scared?" she asked.

"Because I don't want to disappoint you," he said to her. "I want you to trust me."

"There's no one I trust more, you won't disappoint me," she said and ran her hands over his chest.

Kenny turned her around again and untied the back of her petticoat letting it fall on the floor of the wagon with her dress, this time when he turned her back to face him, she was naked. "Your absolutely beautiful," he said as he looked at her. Callie blushed and just grinned at him. Once again Kenny pulled her to him, letting his chest and hers press together skin to skin. He kissed her again, thrusting his tongue into her mouth as he ran his hands over her back and down to her buttocks. Finally, he broke the kiss and helped her lay back on the thin mattress they used at night.

Callie laid on top of the quilt as she watched Kenny pull off first his boots and then his britches. His cock popped straight out when it was uncovered, the size of it made her gasp. Once he was naked too, he laid down on the quilt next to her, noticing her eyes still stayed on his cock.

"You can touch it if you want," he said to her.

82

"Are you sure?" she said, reaching out and running the tip of one finger down the side.

"I'm sure," he said, putting his hand on top of hers so that she had to take it in her hand. He began moving her hand up and down, showing her how to stroke him.

"It's soft and hard," she said, "but bigger than I thought it would be."

"I'll try to be gentle," he said as he again began kissing her. Callie wrapped her arms around his neck as he rolled her onto her back and leaned over her.

With one arm being used to hold him up, he let the other roam down the front of her, letting it play with her breasts before letting it slide lower to her stomach. When Callie didn't complain he let his hand slide lower until it sat on top of the hair that covered her muff.

"Spread your legs," he said to her, and she did, just enough for him to slide his fingers into her folds, where he found her already becoming wet.

He let his fingers slide down and gather some of the moisture before bringing them back up to her clit. He let his fingers slide back and forth over it until he felt it begin to harden. He moved his mouth down to her neck first where he licked and sucked, before moving back to her breasts. Callie began panting and moaned once more, louder this time.

"Shh," he told her, fighting back a grin.

He reached over and took one of the pieces of linen that Callie kept handy for various things, and he slid it under her hips and thighs. Not wanting her virgin blood to get on the mattress or quilt.

"What's that for?" Callie asked.

"You'll see," Kenny said, not wanting to scare her.

He leaned over her once again and sucked on a breast while he ran his fingers over her clit. He moved his fingers lower again and found her plenty wet enough. He gathered more moisture and moved his finger back to her clit where he began rubbing more vigorously as he moved himself between her legs. He let his mouth latch onto her breast again as she started lifting her hips just a little to increase the friction from his fingers.

Callie wasn't sure what was happening to her, but she knew she didn't want it to stop. When Kenny first touched her down below the waist she wasn't sure what she was supposed to do, but he'd started rubbing on a place she never even knew about, and it seemed to send a wonderful tingling sensation through every part of her body. She may not know what was happening, but she knew she needed him to push down on that spot just a little harder and she started pushing her hips towards his hand to make it happen. She felt Kenny's fingers slide down lower and felt one push up inside her as he replaced one nipple in his mouth with the other. Soon she was lifting her hips again trying to make his finger go deeper.

Kenny pulled his finger out of her and let his cock slide through her folds from her clit to her opening getting her used to it. Once she seemed relaxed, he lined his cock up with her opening, and pushed forward until just the head of it was inside her.

"Are you alright?" he asked, pushing forward just a little more.

"Yes," Callie said, "don't stop."

"I wasn't planning on it," he said as he pushed forward just a bit more until he felt the barrier inside her. He took her breast in his hand and began rolling her nipple between his finger and thumb until it again hardened. He leaned forward and just before he clamped his mouth over hers he said, "I'm sorry." He then thrust his hips forward, breaking through her barrier and seating himself fully inside her.

Callie felt a tearing inside her as Kenny drove his cock up into her. She tried to bring her hands up and push him away but couldn't get her arms between them. She let out a small scream which Kenny muffled with his kiss.

"Stop," she said, turning her head to the side.

"Don't move," he said to her. "I know it hurt, but it never will again."

"How do you know?" she asked, wanting to cry. Everything had felt so good up until now.

"My Papa told me," he said to her. "Boys talk to their Papa's just like girls talk to their Mama's." He didn't say anything else for a minute, then asked, "how do you feel now? Does it still hurt?"

"No," Callie said, a bit surprised. "Was that it? Are we done?"

"No," Kenny said and held back his laugh.

He pulled his cock out just a small ways and then slowly pushed it back in. Callie winced a little but didn't seem to be in pain. He pulled back and pushed back again, getting the same result.

"Does it still hurt?" he asked.

"Not really," Callie said, "it just feels strange."

"Let me know if it starts to hurt again," he said, this time pulling almost all the way out before pushing his hips forward until he was deep inside her. He began doing it over and over again. Soon Callie started pushing her hips towards him, trying to get him to go deeper. Kenny knew he wouldn't last much longer, he again reached down between them and played with her hardened clit. He rubbed back and forth over it until he felt her muff begin to tighten around him. He took her clit between his fingers and gave it a good squeeze as he again brought his mouth down on hers to muffle her cries. He plunged his cock into her tight muff a few more times before erupting inside of her.

Kenny waited a few seconds and caught his breath before rolling off and lying on the bed next to her. Neither of them spoke for a minute as they caught their breath.

"Kenny?" Callie said.

"What?" Kenny asked.

"How often do married people do that?" she asked.

"I don't know," he said, "I've never been married before."

"Do you think they do it every day?" she asked.

"I hope so," he said and grinned at her as he got up and grabbed a damp cloth out of a bucket he'd put in the wagon earlier.

"Me too," Callie said and laughed. "What are you doing?"

"Cleaning you up," Kenny said to her as he pulled the piece of linen out from under her, Callie wasn't surprised to see blood on it.

"My Mama told me that would happen," she said, remembering that conversation, but still a little embarrassed.

"It's something to be proud of, Callie," Kenny said as he began wiping her thighs.

"I can do it," she said reaching for the cloth.

"I've got it," Kenny said, finishing what he was doing and lying back down next to her. He reached over and slid an arm under Callie, rolling her onto her side and pulling her over to lay her head on his chest. "Get some sleep now, wife," he said softly, kissing the top of her head.

Callie just nodded as she began to doze off with her arm over his chest. Kenny smiled as he too fell asleep.

Callie was sure he was sleeping when she whispered, "I love you, Kenny Johnson."

**********

Kenny woke the next morning before the sound of the bugle. He'd slept well. He looked down at Callie who was still asleep with her head on his chest. He carefully rolled her onto her back and scooted down to the end of the mattress. He hoped Callie liked the way he was about to wake her up. He gently pulled the quilt off of her legs before carefully spreading them apart. He settled his torso between her thighs so that he was looking straight down at her muff.

"What are you doing," Callie mumbled, barely awake.

"Don't move," he said to her, giving the inside of her thigh a little pinch, which made her clamp her hand over her mouth to quiet the squeal that came out. "I think you're going to like this."

He took one side of her muff in each hand and pulled it apart, exposing her clit and opening to him. He lowered his head and let his tongue flick her clit over and over again until it again began to harden. He knew he didn't have much time, so he moved quicker than he wanted to. He pushed one finger into her already wet opening and began working it in and out at the same rhythm as his tongue flicked her clit.

Callie let out a moan, and Kenny told her teasingly, "you have to be quiet now. You don't want to wake everyone." Callie lifted the quilt they used at night and bit down on it trying to stifle the sounds she was making. Kenny grinned and went back to what he was doing. Soon Callie felt a flutter in her belly as her body again erupted in pleasure. Kenny crawled over her and entered her fully with one thrust.

"No pain today?" he asked, not moving.

"Just a pinch," Callie said, "mostly it feels good."

87

Kenny worked up a much faster rhythm then he had the night before. He pulled his cock all the way out before pushing it much for forcefully back into her. He went faster and faster, and Callie lifted her hips and met him each time. Soon he felt her muff grip his cock tight as she orgasmed a second time, Kenny joined her a few thrusts later.

"You make too much noise, wife," Kenny teased as he laid down next to her. "I might just have to gag you next time."

"Do people do that?" Callie asked curiously.

"I've heard of it being done," he said to her and chuckled.

Before Callie could ask any more questions, the sound of the bugle echoed through the camp letting them know it was time to get up and continue their journey west.

"How do you feel?" Kenny asked her as he got up and held out his hand to her.

"Like a real wife," she said, smiling at him as she placed her hand in his, "finally."

# Chapter 8. Half-way

"We'll be stopping at Independence rock tonight," Harley said as he rode up to the side of the wagon. "We'll make camp there for a couple of days."

"Doesn't that mean we're half-way to Oregon now?" Kenny asked.

"Sure does," Harley said, "and we're making good time. We've only had a few bad weather days to slow us down. Do you know why they call it Independence Rock?"

"Not really," Kenny answered.

"It's where you want to be around Independence Day," Harley explained.

"That's not for more than another week," Callie said, "unless I've lost track of my days."

"You're right, little lady," Harley told her. "That's why we can afford to stay two or three nights. We'll let the animals have a good rest and eat their fill before we move on. The second part of the trail is more difficult, becausefinding grazing land for the animals can be more difficult. "

"You think we might get to Oregon City early?" Kenny asked.

"I'm guessing the middle to end of September if all goes well," Harley answered. "We've still got a long way to go though, so I'm not counting on it."

"That's another three months," Callie said, "we've made it this far in just over two."

"Getting through the Rockies always slows us down, but if we can get there before any snow falls, that would help," Harley told them. "I can't predict the weather, but so far it's been on our side."

"Thanks, Harley," Kenny said as Harley rode off to the next wagon to deliver the message.

"I can't believe we've made it this far," Callie said.

"Don't get too excited," Kenny told her, "we've still got a long way to go."

"I know, but at least we're closer to Oregon than we are to Independence," Callie said.

"You sound almost excited," Kenny joked. "What happened to the girl that didn't want to go to Oregon?"

"She's accepted her fate," Callie said, grinning, "might as well make the best of it."

"Oh really," Kenny said and laughed out loud as he poked her in the side, making her giggle.

"Tell me about your land you bought in Oregon," Callie said, enjoying their conversation and not wanting it to end.

"Our land," Kenny said to her.

"Our land," she repeated and smiled over at him. "Tell me about it."

"I'll let you in on a secret that only Henry and Nick know," Kenny said. "I bought more than one plot."

"Why?" Callie asked.

"I had the money from the sale of Papa's farm," he explained. "When we went to the land office there were eight plots all connected to each other. We bought seven of them and Nick bought the other."

"What are you going to do with all of it?" Callie asked.

"One will belong to Henry," he explained, "and I'll give one to Eddie when he's old enough. I'm hoping Michelle will want to stay close and stay on a piece after she marries."

"That's only three," Callie said, "what about the rest?"

"There's one just in case Lily decides to come west," Kenny said, "although I don't know how she'd get here now."

"They say the railroads will travel all the way out here one day," Callie said to him. "Papa said he'd heard talk of the government building it."

"I hope so," Kenny said, a bit sad, "I hate the thought of never seeing her again. The other three I was planning on keeping for myself. I told you Nick, Henry and me are going to try raising cattle."

"You said was planning. Have you changed your mind?" Callie asked.

"How would you feel about me offering to sell one to your Mama and Papa?" Kenny asked. "That way they'll still be close to you."

"You'd really do that?" Callie asked. "Your family and Nick won't mind?"

"Of course I would," Kenny said. "My family and Nick won't mind, we've all lost our parents; you should be close to yours."

"Tell me more about Nick," Callie said. "Why didn't he come west when you did?"

"Nick Garrett has been my best friend since we started school together. You'll like him. He couldn't leave when we did because he was waiting for his farm to sell," Kenny explained. "His parents died a few years ago. His Papa was sick for a long time, but after he passed on, his Mama just gave up. She died a few months later."

"What if he can't sell it?" Callie asked.

"It was already sold," Kenny said. "There was a telegram from him waiting for us in Independence when we arrived. He

91

said he had the money and would be on his way soon. I'm sure he's already on the trail."

"I hope his train is having as good of luck as ours," she answered. "Is that it?" she asked, half standing up as she pointed at a large rock way off in the distance, it looked more like a big hill.

"I think so," Kenny answered.

"How long do you think it'll take us to get there?" Callie asked.

"Probably a couple more hours," Kenny answered as they both settled back into a comfortable silence.

**********

"Look," Callie said, "there are other people here."

"Looks like another wagon train," Kenny said, "not as big as ours though."

It wasn't the first time they'd seen another wagon train heading west, but they'd never seen one like this. The people were loud and boisterous, yelling and waving their hats as the wagons in Harley's train rolled past. Off behind the wagons, she could see men racing horses across the prairie as others cheered them on.

"They seem a bit rowdy," Callie said as she looked over the already set up camp. Harley kept them moving forward as they looked for a flat, open place to set up their own.

She looked again near the wagons and saw men that were sitting around playing cards while they gulped down shots of whatever liquor was in the bottle that sat on the table. Callie was a bit surprised to see they all wore guns strapped to their waist. There didn't seem to be many women with them, and the ones that were, wore dresses so low cut Callie could see the top of their breasts. Their faces were painted with makeup, and they blew kisses at some of the men as they went by.

"Whoa," Kenny said pulling back on the reins, stopping the oxen.

"Why are we stopping?" Callie asked.

"One of the men just stopped Harley, and they're talking," Kenny said, leaning out the side of the wagon to see what was happening.

"I wonder what they want?" Callie asked, a bit nervous, "I don't know if these are trustworthy people from the look of them."

"I don't know," Kenny said, "but Harley's shaking his head, so whatever it is, he said no."

Soon the wagons began moving again as the men and women from the other train stood watching them go by. One of the card players looked right at Callie and winked at her. Callie didn't like the smile that appeared on his face; it wasn't sincere. Harley led them another half mile down the trail before having the wagons circle and make camp.

The Johnsons and Fishers worked well together after all this time. Henry, Kenny and Norman unhitched the oxen and took them down to the river to drink their fill before putting them out in the field to graze. Callie and Michelle began collecting wood and buffalo chips to make a fire, while Eddie dug a shallow hole and lined it with rocks for a firepit. Nellie pulled out the crates and boards they used to set up a table. Soon their camp was set.

"Looks like we'll be neighbors the next few days," Reverend Drews said as he unloaded his wagon next to the Fishers.

"Why don't you and Julia join us for supper tonight, Reverend?" Nellie offered.

"You sure it's not too much trouble?" Reverend Drews asked.

"Not at all," Nellie said, "you're both more than welcome."

93

"We'd like that," Reverend Drews answered. "We'll be over after we get camp set up."

"Take your time," Nellie told him. "It'll be nice to stay in one place for a few days."

"That it will," Julia Drews said as she walked around the wagon, her baby bump more noticeable now.

"I just invited you both to supper tonight," Nellie said to her.

"Please tell me you accepted?" Julia said to her husband who nodded at her. "Praise the Lord."

**\*\*\*\*\*\*\*\*\*\***

"Howdy," Harley said as he joined them at their fire later that day.

"Howdy, Harley," Norman answered, "can I interest you in a cup of coffee?"

"Don't mind if I do," Harley said, waiting until Nellie filled a cup and handed it to him before finding a seat on a stool.

"I'm looking forward to a few days of rest," Nellie said to him. "I've got some washing and mending that needs to be done. I tried doing my mending in the back of the wagon, but I kept stabbing my finger while I was being bumped around."

"Not much you can get done in a moving wagon," Harley agreed. "I did stop for a reason though."

"What's that?" Kenny asked.

"I'm just warning everyone to keep their women-folk in sight," Harley said, "I don't like the look of some of those gentlemen in the train that was here already."

"We noticed them playing cards and drinking," Callie said.

"They stopped me and asked if we'd like to share their camp," Harley said, "but I told them we'd rather look after ourselves."

"I'm glad you did," Kenny said, then he looked at Callie and Michelle, "you heard what he said, no wandering off alone." They both nodded at him.

"Did you see the dresses the women were wearing?" Michelle asked. "I wonder where they came from that the women dress like that?"

"My guess, little lady, is that those are women who work in houses of ill repute," Harley said.

"What's a house of ill repute?" Eddie asked.

"Not god fearing women," Nellie said.

"Most of those women have had tough lives," Reverend Drews said, "I try not to judge them."

"You're a good man, Reverend," Harley said.

"And they're all going west?" Callie asked.

"Men outnumber women ten to one out there," Harley said and shrugged.

"You mean they're going there to work?" Nellie asked.

"That would be my guess," Harley said, "there's a lot of mining towns springing up all over Oregon and California. Plenty of saloons are looking for women like that."

"Is Oregon City a mining town?" Callie asked.

"No," Harley answered. "There's a lot of families settling around there; it's more a farming community."

"Do you think I should go talk to them?" Reverend Drews asked.

"I wouldn't if you want to sleep inside the wagon tonight," Julia said seriously at first but grinned when Harley laughed so hard he sprayed coffee into the fire.

"I also wanted to let you know that a lot of people like to climb the rock and carve their names in it," Harley said, trying to compose himself, "it's become a bit of a tradition."

"Can we climb it?" Eddie asked, becoming excited.

"Tomorrow after breakfast," Henry answered, "we all can."

"I think I'll sit this one out," Nellie told them.

"I'll stay and keep you company," Norman said, glad for a reason to be able to stay by the wagon and rest.

\*\*\*\*\*\*\*\*\*\*

"Harder, Kenny," Callie whispered as Kenny pumped his cock in and out of her. She was on her hands and knees while Kenny knelt behind her. Every night it seemed they tried something new, but this position was her favorite so far.

Kenny gripped her hips and pumped into her as fast and hard as he could until he felt Callie's muff begin to squeeze his cock so tight it was almost difficult to pull it out. He plunged into her just a few more times before he too climaxed.

Callie collapsed naked on her stomach on their bedding as Kenny laid down next to her. "It just gets better every time," he finally said once he caught his breath.

"I don't think it can get much better than that," Callie said and giggled.

"I'll have to see what I can come up with for tomorrow," Kenny said jokingly. He reached over and pulled Callie back against him and threw the quilt over them. "Good night, wife," he said, kissing the back of her neck.

"Good night, husband," Callie said. She laid there for quite a while not able to go to sleep. Every night she waited until Kenny was asleep to tell him she loved him, but she didn't want to do that anymore. Finally, she asked, "Kenny, are you still awake?"

"What's wrong?" he asked.

"I need to tell you something," she said to him.

"Go ahead," he told her.

"I'm scared," she admitted.

"Did something happen?" he asked.

"No," she said.

"Just tell me, Callie," he encouraged her.

"Alright," she said and took a deep breath, "I love you."

Kenny wasn't sure how to respond. He stayed quiet for a minute thinking about what he wanted to say. Did he love Callie? He still wasn't sure. Was he dishonoring Sadie if he told another woman he loved her? Even if that woman was his wife?

"Aren't you going to say anything?" Callie asked.

"Callie, I..," Kenny was speechless. "I don't know how I feel. I know I like you, and I want you with me."

"That's all you have to say?" Callie asked.

"Callie, you have to understand," Kenny tried to explain.

"Nevermind," Callie said and pulled the quilt up to her chin.

"I've told you before; I'm not good with words," Kenny said.

"It doesn't matter," Callie said sadly, closing her eyes and not saying anything else.

Kenny laid back quietly not saying anything himself, knowing that tonight Callie wasn't going to say 'I love you' like she said to him every night once she thought he was asleep. He was pretty sure his wife cried herself to sleep that night.

**********

Callie climbed out of the wagon early the next morning as the sun was beginning to rise. Since they were resting for a few days, there wouldn't be a bugle sounding before sunrise and waking them up. She hadn't been able to sleep most of the night anyway. She just needed some time alone to think.

Even though Kenny had told her multiple times not to leave the camp, she began walking, thinking about what was said, or not said, the night before. She knew she loved Kenny, but could she be happy knowing he might never love her back? This thought troubled her.

Callie was so deep in thought she didn't pay attention to where she was going or how far from camp she was getting. Before she realized it, she was on the edge of the wagon train camp that was there when they arrived the day before.

"Well hello there," one of the men said as he approached her. It was the same man that winked at her the day before as they rode past. "I remember you."

"I'm sorry," Callie said, backing up a step. "I wasn't paying attention; I didn't mean to intrude."

"Well ain't she a pretty one, Joe," another man said.

"She sure is, Leroy," the one named Joe answered. "Why don't you come have a seat and be neighborly." The man was smiling, but it wasn't a friendly smile. "Looks like we're all out of extra chairs, but you can sit on my lap."

"No thank you," Callie said nervously, "I really must be getting back." She took another step backward as the two men grinned at her.

"What's your hurry," a voice said from behind her as a hand came down on each of her shoulders.

"Take your hands off me," Callie said and tried to shrug them off.

"That's not too friendly of you," the voice behind her said, giving her shoulders a squeeze. "My friends over there invited you to stay for a bit, even offered you a seat."

"Let me go," Callie said again, trying to pull away.

"She's a feisty one, Joe, can we keep her?" the voice behind her said as he tightened his grip again.

"Let's see if she's worth keeping first," Joe answered, beginning to stand up.

Callie was trying not to panic, but she wasn't sure what to do next. She again tried to pull away as the men from the fire walked towards her.

"Mister," she heard Kenny say, "if you don't take your hands off my wife, I'm gonna shoot ya."

**********

Kenny heard Callie get up and leave the wagon. He wasn't sure what to say to her after last night. He felt like a jerk. He waited a few minutes for her to return, knowing they needed to talk. He thought about what he wanted to say to her. He knew he cared for her a great deal, and he needed her to know that. After a bit of time, he began to wonder if she was even coming back.

He heard Nellie and Norman come out of their wagon and get the fire started. They talked quietly to each other as Nellie started brewing their morning coffee. He wondered if Callie was pouting when he didn't hear her voice. He finally decided to get up and join them. He threw on his britches and a clean shirt before climbing out of the wagon.

"Good morning," he said to Nellie and Norman.

"Good morning," Nellie answered. "Callie sleeping in this morning?"

"She's been up for at least a quarter of an hour now," Kenny said, looking around. "You haven't seen her?"

"Did she go to see to her personal needs?" Nellie asked.

"She knows better than to go too far with those other people around," Kenny said.

"Coffee?" Norman asked.

"Thank you," Kenny said and took a cup from him.

"Good morning," Henry said as he crawled out from under the second wagon.

"You know we could always make you up a bed in the wagon," Kenny said, a bit guilty that he had a bed every night while his brother slept under the wagon Michelle slept in.

"Don't worry about it," Henry told him. "I sleep pretty well most night."

"If you change your mind, just speak up," Kenny said.

"Where's Callie?" Henry asked, pouring himself a cup from the pot near the fire, "still sleeping?"

"No," Kenny said, looking around, "and I'm getting worried."

"You don't think something's happened to her do you?" Norman asked.

"I don't know, Norman," Kenny said, walking to the back of the wagon and grabbing his rifle out of it. "But I'm going to find out. If she wandered away from this camp, I swear I'm gonna spank her till she can't sit down."

"Why would she wander off?" Nellie asked.

"She was a bit upset with me," Kenny answered, "but that's no reason to leave camp."

"She's always gone for a walk when she needs to think through her troubles," Nellie said, wringing her hands and looking from Kenny to Norman.

"I'll go with you," Norman said as he too grabbed his rifle. Henry didn't say anything but grabbed his own and joined his brother, nodding at him.

"There a problem, folks?" Harley asked, walking over to them. "Makes me nervous when I see people grabbing guns this early in the morning."

100

"Callie's missing," Kenny said, "may be nothing, but I'm not taking any chances."

"Hold on a minute," Harley said and quickly went back to his wagon, calling out to a few others on the way. By the time he returned just a few minutes later, he had his own rifle. Reverend Drews was with him and was also armed, as were a few others. "Let's go."

"Reverend?" Nellie said, looking at the gun in his hands.

"I'll be trying to end things peacefully, but that doesn't mean I won't protect myself or our women folk," Reverend Drews said as he followed the rest of the men.

They decided the first place they'd look was at the other camp. Kenny walked quickly as they made their way there, he had a bad feeling, and was sure he wasn't going to like what he found there. When he rounded the last turn on the trail, he saw red as two men stood in front of his wife, while another man stood behind her with his hands on her, holding her in place. Callie looked scared.

Kenny raised his gun to his shoulder and walked towards the men, saying, "mister, if you don't take your hands off my wife, I'm gonna shoot ya."

"Easy now, we don't want any trouble. My names Joe, and I run this here wagon train," one of the men in front of Callie said as he raised his hands, motioning for the other two to do the same.

"Joe," Kenny just about snarled, "tell your man there to take his hands off my wife."

"She wandered into our camp," Joe said, as he motioned for the man to take his hands off Callie. "We were just seeing if she needed any help getting back to yours."

"She doesn't need your help," Kenny assured him, as Callie rushed over to join Kenny and her Papa. "I'll escort my wife back."

"Of course," Joe said, giving a snakey smile. "Come back and visit us any time, Mrs…?"

"You don't need to know her name," Kenny said, tucking Callie in behind him, "you won't be seeing her again."

"No need to be rude," Joe said, "we were just trying to be neighborly."

"I'm sure you were," Kenny said sarcastically. "We'll be taking our leave now."

Kenny walked backwards keeping his eyes on the men as the group turned and headed back to their own camp. He didn't turn around until he was sure they were out of the men's sight.

"Are you alright?" Norman asked Callie.

"I'm fine, Papa," Callie answered, still a bit shaken. "I just need to sit down when we get back to camp."

"You enjoy that sit," Kenny just about growled at her, "I don't think you'll want to sit again for the rest of the day after I'm finished with you."

"Kenny," Callie protested and stumbled. "I'm sorry."

"You're going to be sorrier," he said, taking her gently by the arm so she wouldn't fall.

"Me and Henry will take Eddie and Michelle down to the river to give you a bit of privacy," Norman said.

"Papa," Callie again protested.

"Those men could of hurt you, Callie," Norman said. "If your Mama would have wandered off, I'd be taking my belt to her."

"No you wouldn't," Callie said. "You'd never spank Mama."

"Girl," Norman said, a bit angry with her now that he knew she was safe, "when your mama and me first married, I turned her over my knee plenty."

Callie didn't say anything else, she knew she'd done wrong. Instead, she started thinking about how she could talk Kenny out of it, or if that was even possible.

# Chapter 9. A Reckoning

"Is everyone done?" Nellie asked, looking at her daughter who sat quietly at the table finishing her breakfast. Norman and Kenny explained what had happened to all of them when they'd returned, Callie hadn't said much.

"I think we're all finished," Kenny answered.

"There are a few biscuits left if anyone wants another," Michelle told them.

"I can't eat another bite," Henry said, patting his stomach. "You sure are becoming a good cook, Michelle."

"Nellie's taught me about cooking over a fire," Michelle said, smiling at the older woman who treated her more like a daughter every day.

"That's good," Henry told her, "you'll be cooking over a fire for a while longer until we can get a house built."

"How long do you think that'll take?" Michelle asked.

"At least a month," Kenny answered, "maybe longer. We'll put in an order for lumber as soon as we get there, but I don't know how long it'll take to fill our order."

"What'll we do while we wait?" Michelle asked.

"The land needs to be cleared where we want to build," Kenny explained. "That'll take us some time. Henry wants a log cabin made from the trees we cut down. We can always start that. There'll be plenty to do to keep us busy."

"Can I help?" Eddie asked.

"Of course you can," Henry said, "the more everyone pitches in, the faster we get it done."

"Where will we stay while you build it?" Michelle asked.

"In the wagons," Kenny answered, "that's why we need to get one finished as quickly as possible. Henry can't be sleeping under the wagon when winter starts."

"He could sleep in the wagon," Michelle said, "there's room."

"I'm fine where I am," Henry said to them. "Don't worry about me."

"Nellie, do you need Callie to finish anything for you this morning? Once we go to the wagon, she won't be coming out for the rest of the day," Kenny said.

"Kenny," Callie began to protest.

"Not another word," Kenny said to her. "We'll talk in the wagon."

"Why can't we talk right here?" Callie asked, knowing she wasn't going to like the answer.

"Because while we're talking, you'll be over my knee," he said to her quietly, so only those at their table would hear. "Would you like me to do that out here, where everyone can see?"

"I don't want you to do it at all," Callie said to him, "it's not like I wandered into their camp on purpose."

"You knew you weren't supposed to wander away at all," Kenny said, standing up.

"I needed to think," Callie started to explain. "I didn't mean to go so far from camp."

"Nellie?" Kenny said, lifting an eyebrow at his mother-in-law.

"Michelle will help me with the dishes," Nellie said, nodding at him, although she did frown a bit. "Eddie and Henry can help Norman take the oxen down to the river for a drink."

"I appreciate that," Kenny said nodding at her.

"Kenny," Callie tried to say again, but he cut off her words.

"You want to talk," Kenny said, "so let's go talk in private."

"I don't want to go to the wagon to talk," Callie said, standing up and crossing her arms.

"Just remember," Kenny said, grabbing her by the arm as he knelt and pulled her forward over his knee, "you're the one who wanted to talk out here." He brought his hand down on her butt. *Smack, smack, smack, smack, smack, smack.*

"Kenny, stop," Callie hissed, "people are watching."

"Would you like to continue our conversation out here, or go to the wagon?" he asked.

"The wagon," she said quickly as he put her back on her feet. Callie didn't look at anyone as she made her way into the back of the wagon, Kenny was right behind her.

Norman and Nellie both shook their heads as they watched the young couple go. They both knew Callie deserved the spanking she was about to get.

"I can't believe you'd embarrass me like that," Callie said as she turned to face him.

"I can't believe the danger you put yourself in this morning," Kenny calmly said to her, sitting down on a crate.

"I didn't mean to," Callie explained, "I just needed to think and thought I'd walk for a few minutes. I wasn't even paying attention."

"I understand needing time to think," he told her. "I'm sorry about last night, Callie, I know I hurt you with my words."

"You don't have to apologize for your feelings," she said, cutting him off. "You can't help it if you don't love me."

"Callie," he began again, trying to think of a way to explain it to her.

"No, Kenny," she said. "I don't want to talk about it anymore."

"You still have a reckoning coming," he said to her.

"But I explained what happened," she said, "and I apologized."

"You explained you weren't paying attention," he said, reaching out for her and turning her around in front of him. He lifted her skirt and tucked it into the waistband of her dress, surprised to find her not wearing a petticoat. "Do you have any idea what those men could have done to you?"

"Of course I know," Callie answered, trying not to cry thinking about it. "I was scared until you and Papa showed up."

"I'm going to make sure you pay attention for now on," Kenny said, turning her back towards him and flipping her over his knees. "There's a lot of dangers in Oregon; you can't just wander off."

"Stop, Kenny," she said, trying to get up. "Everyone will know what's happening in here."

"They will," he said and began bringing his hand down on both sides of her butt. *Smack, smack, smack, smack, smack, smack, smack, smack, smack, smack.* "They probably all know why it's happening too." *Smack, smack, smack, smack, smack, smack, smack, smack, smack, smack.* "I can't believe you walked away like that." *Smack, smack, smack, smack, smack, smack, smack, smack, smack, smack.* "I'm going to make sure you think about where you're going the next time you want to be alone." *Smack, smack, smack, smack, smack, smack, smack, smack, smack, smack.*

Callie let out a steady stream of, "stop." "That hurts." "Ouch." "Not so hard," and finally, "I'm sorry."

"I'm not done yet," he said to her as he grabbed his Mama's hairbrush out of the trunk next to him. "You'll be thinking about how much danger you put yourself in every time you sit down today." *Splat, splat, splat, splat, splat, splat.*

"That's too much, Kenny," Callie just about screamed.

"Too much would have been what those men were planning to do to you," he said, beginning another round, on her thighs this time. *Splat, splat, splat, splat, splat, splat.* "I was so angry when I saw that man with his hands on you; I wanted to shoot him." *Splat, splat, splat, splat, splat, splat.*

"I was scared," Callie admitted, beginning to cry hard.

"I was terrified for you," Kenny told her. "If they would have done more than touch your shoulders, they'd all be dead now."

"You don't mean that," Callie cried out.

"Of course I do," Kenny said, sitting her up on his lap and making her wince.

"I'm sorry," she said again, resting her head on his chest. "I won't do it again. I didn't mean to do it this time. I just wanted to walk; I always walk when I need to think. Next thing I knew, I was walking into their camp."

"I know you didn't mean to go there," Kenny said, "but you'll spend the rest of the day in the wagon thinking about what could have happened."

"I can't stay in here all day," she protested. "What am I supposed to do?"

"We're not done yet, Callie," he said to her. "I think you'll be happy to stay in here and rest today. I just thought you could use a break. You've got fifteen strokes with my belt coming yet."

"I won't be able to sit if you do that," Callie answered.

"No," Kenny agreed, "you won't, and for the next few days, you'll think about your safety everytime you sit down."

"Please, Kenny," Callie said, "no more."

"Don't argue, Callie," he said, standing her up and turning her so that she faced the crate, while he stood as well as he could behind her. "Bend over and put your hands on the crate. Arguing will make it twenty strokes."

Callie was shaking as she bent forward and put her hands on the wood box in front of her. She realized there was no talking him out of it. He was right; things could have ended much worse. She closed her eyes as she heard Kenny slide his belt out of the loops on his pants.

"Don't move," he said to her, putting his hand in the middle of her back to calm her.

"Kenny," she started to say as he brought his arm back and delivered the first stroke. *Swish, thwack.* She gasped as it landed.

"I want you to count them," Kenny said to her.

"Why?" she asked, fighting back a new batch of tears.

*Swish, thwack.* "They don't count until you do," Kenny said.

"Two," Callie just about screamed out.

"That was one," he said, "you didn't count the other."

Callie groaned and gritted her teeth as the next stroke landed. *Swish, thwack.* "Two," she yelled out.

Callie counted each stroke as it fell, but by the time they got to the tenth one, she was crying so hard Kenny could barely understand her. He knew he needed to finish this quickly, but what he really wanted to do was stop and hold her in his arms. "You don't have to count anymore," he said. "I'm going to give you the last five quickly so we can finish this." *Swish, thwack. Swish, thwack. Swish, thwack. Swish, thwack. Swish, thwack.*

He let Callie stand where she was as he put his belt back on. Once he was done, he reached over and helped her up, turning her around and pulling her into his arms.

"I didn't enjoy that," he said to her, rubbing her back, "but I'll do it again if need be."

Callie just nodded as she returned his embrace. He again sat down on the crate and pulled her towards him. "I can't sit," she said, not wanting him to pull her onto his lap.

"I know," Kenny said, "but I can't stand up straight in this dang wagon. How about if I help you lie down, and you take a bit of a nap? You look tired, Callie."

Callie nodded at him; she was tired. The months of walking every day had made her strong, but the constant work and lack of sleep the night before were catching up to her. Kenny helped her lie down and stroked her head and back as she cried. "Callie," he finally said. "I'm sorry about last night."

"I don't want to talk about it anymore," Callie said, closing her eyes.

"Just let me say this, and we'll not talk about it again," he said to her. "I do care for you, more than I thought I'd ever care for another woman again. When I tell you I love you, I want to mean it. Not just say it to make you happy. Does that make sense to you?"

"I'd like you to mean it too," Callie said as she drifted off, exhausted after the spanking she'd just received.

\*\*\*\*\*\*\*\*\*\*

"Wake up sleepy head," she heard Kenny say as he woke her. "You've been sleeping all day."

"I have?" she asked as she sat up gingerly. Although her bottom still hurt a little, it was nothing like it hurt when Kenny first finished.

110

"I thought you might be hungry," he said as he held a plate up in front of her.

"I'm starving," she said to him. "I should've helped Mama and Michelle get supper together."

"Your Mama knows what happened this morning," Kenny told her. "She understands why you're not out there with everyone."

"Does everyone know you spanked me?" she asked as she began eating.

"Did everyone know when Mr. Evans spanked his wife last week? Or when Mr. Lightner spanked his the week before?" Kenny asked and tried to hide his grin.

"It's not funny, Kenny. I guess they all know," Callie said, her cheeks turning red as she took another bite of the stew her mama and Michelle cooked.

"You're right; it's not. Callie, no one will care," Kenny said. "I wouldn't worry about it."

"I'm embarrassed to see everyone tomorrow," Callie said truthfully.

"Why?" Kenny said, sitting on the thin mattress next to her.

"Because they may not care," she said, "but I do."

"In a few days, half of the people on the trail will have forgotten about what happened between us," Kenny told her. Then to change the subject he asked, "you gonna be up for a walk to the top of Independence Rock tomorrow?"

"Didn't you go today?" she asked him.

"No," he said shaking his head and taking the empty dish from her and setting it down behind him. "Henry took Michelle and Eddie up earlier, but I wanted to wait for you. We have to carve our names into the rock."

"I'm glad you waited," she said and smiled at him.

111

Kenny leaned down and kissed her. "Are we alright?" he asked her.

"What do you mean?" she asked.

"After what happened last night?" he said. "I meant what I said earlier, Callie. I want to mean those words when I say them to you."

"And if you never say them?" she asked, a bit sadly.

"I don't think you have to worry about that," he said, trying to reassure her.

Callie wrapped her arms around his neck and pulled him down to kiss her again. Kenny put an arm around her back and pulled her towards him, slipping his tongue into her mouth as he ran his hand up and down her back.

"Do you have to go back to the fire?" she asked him. She didn't know why, but she needed him. If he couldn't love her with his mind, he could still love her with his body.

"No," he answered, watching as she pulled her dress over her head, leaving her naked on the bed.

Kenny jumped up and made sure the wagon cover was tied tightly shut before pulling his shirt and britches off. He laid back down on the bed next to her. He reached out for her, but she stopped him by putting a hand on his chest. She pushed him down on his back as she got on her knees, taking his cock in her hand. She began stroking him slowly, squeezing as she stroked upward until a drop of liquid formed at the tip. She leaned forward and licked it off. Kenny let out a soft groan.

Callie leaned forward and sucked his cock into her mouth, just the way he'd shown her how. She pulled back and then sucked him in even further.

"That feels so good," Kenny said, propping himself up on his elbow so he could watch. He reached out with his other hand and cupped the back of her head. "Don't stop."

Callie worked up a rhythm. As she sucked his cock, she flicked her tongue in all the places she knew he liked. Kenny began to breathe heavier as he cupped her head even tighter. Callie glanced up at him and grinned before letting her mouth slide off of him with a pop. She licked around the top and up and down the side of it before pulling it back into her mouth. Kenny felt his balls tighten and gripped her head harder as he erupted in her mouth. Something he'd only done once before. Callie swallowed it all down before licking him one last time and sitting back on her heels.

"Your turn," Kenny said, sitting up quickly, grabbing her under the arms, pulling her down on top of him, and then flipping them both over so that he was on top. He did it so fast Callie didn't have time to protest, but did let out a squeal, and then giggled.

Kenny began kissing her neck first. He licked and sucked behind her ears and slowly worked his way down to her chest. He pulled first one nipple and then the other into his mouth as he rolled the other between his finger and thumb. He bit down on one just a bit before letting it go and moving lower. He ran his tongue over her breast, down her stomach, to the hair that covered her muff. He didn't give her time to think. He pushed her legs up and hooked them over his shoulders. He forced her legs far enough apart that her muff parted on its own, exposing her most sensitive parts to him. Kenny could tell she was already wet. He blew on her clit softly before lowering his head and licking her from opening to clit, over and over again, until he felt it begin to harden. He took one of his fingers and pushed it up inside of her; her juices

113

dripped down onto his hand, he pulled that one finger out and replaced it with two.

Kenny glanced up and had to grin as he saw Callie had the quilt once again clenched between her teeth to keep from crying out. Her eyes were tightly closed as she squirmed underneath him.

He pulled his fingers out of her and pushed his tongue as far up into her as he could, thrusting it in and out as he let his finger slide down to her bottom hole. He let his wet fingers rub all around it before beginning to work one up inside of her. Callie let out another squeal but didn't protest; Kenny felt his cock harden again.

Once he worked his finger as far up into her bottom as he could get it, he moved his tongue back to her clit. Licking it continuously as he started pumping his finger in and out of her. Soon her clit hardened even more, and it began to pulse under his tongue. He slowed his motions down until he felt her relax.

Kenny climbed over her and put a hand down on each side of her head; he was looking into her eyes as he entered her; sinking his cock into her slowly. Once he was in as far as he could go, he again wrapped his arms around her and flipped them both over, so she was on top of him.

Callie put her hands on his chest and began lifting herself up and then sinking back down on him. The two kept their eyes locked as she began moving faster and faster, and grinding her hips down harder. Finally, Kenny pulled her towards him, holding her tight as he ground his cock up into her, making them both reach their pleasure together.

Kenny lifted her off and laid her down next to him, pulling her back into his front like he did every night. He was glad everything seemed alright between them after the night before.

"Good night, Kenny," Callie said like she did every night.

"Good night, Callie," he answered.

Kenny laid there silently, waiting until she thought he was asleep so she would say those three words she said every night. Soon he knew Callie was already sleeping. He laid there awake wondering why it bothered him so much that her words never came.

# Chapter 10. Stampede

"We'll be leaving the plains soon," Harley said as they sat around drinking coffee.

"I'll be glad for a change of scenery," Callie said.

"Getting through the Rockies is the worst part of the trip," Harley said, "but once we're through, we'll be in Oregon."

"How much longer?" Nellie asked, looking tired.

"Only about another month," Harley said. "We've made good time. We should get to Oregon City the middle of September."

"That's sooner than I thought we'd get there," Kenny said. "I should have plenty of time to get a house built before winter."

"Winters in Oregon aren't too harsh," Harley said. "You'll be able to build most of the year round."

"What about you, Harley?" Nellie asked. "You have a house already waiting for you?"

"No," he said, "I'll be building myself until Roland gets there."

"How far behind us do you think they are?" Callie asked.

"A month, two at the most," Harley answered. "We've made good time, only hit a couple of storms. The river crossings went easy. We've only lost one wagon, and only two people died. No telling what kind of problems Roland's train might have had."

"I felt so bad for the Baker's when their boy got bit by that rattler and died," Nellie said.

"We all did," Harley told them, "but I've had much worse happen on these trips."

"What's the worse thing that you had happen?" Eddie asked.

"Eddie," Michelle scolded, "that's a terrible thing to ask."

"The boy's just curious," Harley said, "no harm done. I think the worst trip was two years ago; we had an Influenza outbreak. We were stopped for nearly two weeks and lost over thirty people. That was hard. Women left with no husbands; husbands left with no wives, children left without parents. We were lucky and had a doctor traveling with us, without him we would've lost more. That's why I make sure there's one traveling with us every year now."

"That must have been horrible," Callie said.

"It was," Harley agreed. "We ran into some bad weather that year too. A few people turned back when we reached the forts, I don't know what happened to them. Only half the people I started with made it all the way to Oregon."

"I hope the men out hunting make it back soon," Nellie said. "I worry about Norman out after dark."

"They insisted on getting a few more buffalo before we get to the mountains," Harley said, looking west where the outline of the Rockies could be seen. "I thought they'd be back by now."

"I'm wondering how far your land is from ours, Harley," Kenny said.

"My lands a bit southwest of Oregon City," Harley said, "but at the northern end of the Willamette Valley. Close to another two days travel by wagon. The closest town is about an hour away; it's called McMinnville."

"That sounds like it's close to the area we're in," Kenny said. "I remember seeing McMinnville on the map. It'd be nice if we were neighbors."

"That it would," Harley said, "I know Reverend Drews will be living in McMinnville. He told me they opened some kind of school out there, and he was offered a position."

"I like Reverend Drews," Eddie said, "he makes church not so boring."

"Eddie," Michelle again scolded as Henry and Kenny laughed.

"He isn't lying," Henry said when Michelle gave him a dirty look.

"What's that noise?" Nellie asked suddenly.

"What noise?" Kenny asked.

"Don't you hear that rumbling?" Nellie asked them. Everyone sat silently, listening to the rumble off in the distance.

"Sounds like hooves," Harley said, standing up. "Whatever it is, it's coming this way."

They continued to look around as the sound became louder. Soon one of the men that was out hunting, wildly rode into the camp, yelling to Harley, "the buffalo are stampeding, and heading this way."

"What do we do?" Kenny asked, standing up.

"We've got to get them to turn. Get your women in the wagons and come with me," Harley said to the men around him.

"Where's Norman?" Nellie yelled out to the man.

"Trying to get the herd to turn," the man yelled back, then turned his horse and raced back in the other direction.

"Get in the wagon," Kenny said to Callie, Michelle and Nellie. "Don't come out until we come for you." Callie nodded, and Kenny kissed her before running with Henry and Harley towards the buffalo.

"I want to come," Eddie called after them.

"Not this time, squirt," Henry called back to him. "You stay with Michelle."

"Be careful," Callie yelled to them before following the others into the back of the Fisher's wagon.

"I want to go with the men," Eddie said again, still standing near the fire.

"Not this time," Michelle yelled as she waved him over, the sound of the stampeding buffalo getting so loud it was hard to hear above it. "Hurry Eddie!"

Eddie climbed into the wagon with the three woman. He huddled in a corner with Nellie and Michelle while Callie peeked out the back. Soon she could see hundreds of buffalo heading directly towards where the wagons were circled.

Men from the wagon train ran towards them waving blankets and shirts while others on horseback tried to get them to turn. The animals must have seen the wagons ahead of them, blocking their path, and they began to turn on their own to avoid the camp, but the animals on the outside just didn't have enough time.

Callie was still peeking out when the first one ran through the camp, just missing their wagon, but trampling a barrel and knocking down the pot of water that was boiling over the cookfire. Other animals followed, trampling everything in their path.

Callie watched as one of the large animals went by. She'd seen them off in the distance from the wagon, but this was the closest she'd been to one of them. She turned her head to watch the animal run past, not seeing the next as it ran into the side of the wagon. The force of the animal's weight made the wagon slide violently, knocking her off balance, and she fell head first on the ground. The last thing she saw was the large animal turning and barrelling towards her before everything went black.

**\*\*\*\*\*\*\*\*\*\***

Kenny and Henry ran with the rest of the men towards the stampeding herd. They saw Harley take off his shirt and begin waving it in the air as he yelled, they did the same.

"Stay to the side of them," the heard Harley yell, "we have to get them to turn."

The men from the train did everything they could, and were glad to see the animals begin to shift right. Kenny and Henry dove behind a rock to avoid being trampled as the herd went by. Kenny looked forward and seen at least twenty animals crashing through the camp. He began running back towards the wagons, worried about his family.

Norman's wagon came into view just as one of the last in the herd flew past him and smashed into the side. He couldn't believe it when the wagon came at least a foot off the ground before crashing back down. He watched, horrified, as Callie fell out of the back, and hit the ground head first. The buffalo, now confused turned in her direction, he took just a few steps before leaping over her, his hooves just missing her head.

"Callie?" Kenny said as he walked over to her, afraid of what he was going to find. She wasn't moving. "Callie!" he said again as he gathered her into his arms. He felt somewhat relieved when he saw her chest rise and knew she was still breathing.

"Is she alright?" Harley asked, running up to him.

"She hit her head," Kenny explained quickly, "she needs the doctor."

"I'll get him," Henry said, running off.

"What happened?" Norman asked riding up and seeing Kenny holding Callie. "Is she alright?"

"The buffalo ran into the wagon," Nellie explained as she climbed out and ran to her daughter. "Callie was looking out the back. The jolt knocked her out."

"Was she trampled?" Norman asked.

"Didn't look like it," Kenny said, "somehow the buffalo jumped right over her."

"Let's take her to your wagon, Kenny," Nellie said, "we can make her comfortable. Henry should be back with Dr. Martin soon." Kenny nodded at her and carried her towards their wagon, praying she'd be alright.

\*\*\*\*\*\*\*\*\*\*

"She'll be alright," Callie heard Nellie say, "she has to be."

"I can't lose her too," she heard Kenny answer.

"She's strong," Nellie assured him.

"We're going to go back to our wagon for the night," she heard her Papa say, "but if you need us, just holler."

"Thanks, Norman," Kenny answered.

"You don't need to thank me," Norman said, "she may be your wife, but she'll always be my little girl." Callie felt the familiar kiss Norman placed on her forehead.

Callie didn't know why she couldn't seem to open her eyes. Her head was pounding as she listened to what was going on. She felt the wagon sway as Norman climbed down and then helped Nellie.

Once they were alone, Kenny started talking to her. "Please wake up, Callie. Please. I can't lose you too," she heard his voice break, and if she didn't know better, she'd think he was crying. She fell back to sleep with Kenny holding her hand.

\*\*\*\*\*\*\*\*\*\*

121

"The doc says she should wake up soon if she's gonna," Callie heard Kenny say as she once again struggled to open her eyes.

"What if she doesn't?" Michelle asked. "She hit her head hard when she fell. Me and Nellie tried to grab her when we saw her slip, but we weren't fast enough."

"The buffalo jumped right over her," Eddie said, "I was looking out the back. I never saw anything like it."

"She was lucky the damn animal didn't trample her," Kenny said.

"Are you alright, Kenny?" Michelle asked. "You need to get some sleep."

"I can't sleep," Kenny told her. "Every time I close my eyes I see that buffalo jumping over her, and just miss landing on her head."

"Do you love her?" Michelle asked.

"With my whole heart," Kenny whispered, "I just hope she wakes up so I can tell her. Take Eddie and go get some sleep, I'll be fine here."

"You sure?" Michelle asked. "Henry said he'd come sit with you if you want him too."

"I'm sure," Kenny said. "I'll be alright."

Callie fought to open her eyes this time when she felt Michelle and Eddie leave the wagon. At first, everything looked fuzzy, until her eyes focused and then adjusted to the dim light that was coming through the opening in the back of the wagon.

"Did you mean it?" Callie said so quietly Kenny thought he was hearing things until he saw her eyes were open.

"Callie?" Kenny said, clutching her hand, "are you really awake? How do you feel?"

"I'm thirsty," Callie croaked, "can I have something to drink?"

"I've got some water for you right here," Kenny said, helping her sit up and holding the cup to her mouth. She took a big drink.

"Did you mean it?" she asked again as she laid back down.

"Mean what?" Kenny asked, not sure what she was talking about.

"Did you mean it when you told Michelle that you loved me?" she asked him.

"I meant it," Kenny said, "I'm head over heels in love with you, Callie Johnson."

"That's good to know," Callie said, "because I'm head over heels in love with you, Kenny Johnson."

"Good to know," Kenny said, a big smile on his face until he saw Callie wince. "Are you in pain?"

"My head hurts," Callie said to him. "What happened?"

"One of the buffalo ran into the side of Nellie and Norman's wagon. You were looking out the back when it smashed into the side. The wagon moved a good five feet, throwing you out the back. I was just coming back into camp when I saw you fall and that damn buffalo jumped over you. How his hooves didn't come down on top of you, I'll never know."

"Is Mama and Papa's wagon alright?" Callie asked.

"Henry and Norman had to do a few repairs, but it should get them the rest of the way to Oregon," Kenny said.

"No one else was hurt?" Callie asked.

"The only other damage besides you was some trampled pots and pans, a few dirty quilts, and a couple of other wagons, that just like your Mama and Papa's, have already been fixed. We got lucky when most of the herd turned at the last minute," Kenny explained.

"That's good," Callie said, closing her eyes.

"You rest now," Kenny said, pulling her close to him, "I'll watch over you."

"I love you," Callie said again as she relaxed, feeling safe in Kenny's arms. Kenny smiled down at her, not realizing how much he'd missed hearing her say those words.

"Not as much as I love you," Kenny said as he leaned forward and kissed her cheek. He saw Callie grin as she drifted off to sleep. Kenny pulled her in tighter to him, as he too closed his eyes, feeling like he could breathe again.

# Chapter 11. A New Johnson

"Are you sure you're alright?" Kenny asked Callie as he got up and began dressing. "You don't look well." The bugle sounded just a few minutes earlier, waking everyone.

"I'm not feeling my best," Callie admitted before jumping up and barely making it to the back of the wagon before throwing up over the side.

"I'm going to get the doctor," Kenny said, "I'm worried after you hit your head so hard."

"That was two weeks ago, Kenny," Callie said to him. "I think I've just caught a stomach bug. It'll go away in a day or two."

"I'd still like to have the doc look at you," Kenny said to her. "I think you should just stay in bed this morning. Do you want me to bring you some breakfast?"

Just the mention of food made Callie's stomach turn, and she rushed to the edge of the wagon and again got sick over the side.

"Don't even mention food," Callie said, trying not to gag. "I'm just going to lie here for a bit, tell my Mama I'll get up and help her in a few minutes."

"I'm sure Michelle and Nellie can handle breakfast this morning," Kenny said, then felt bad when he saw Callie's face turn a bit green again. "Is there anything I can get you?"

Callie just waved her hand at him and shook her head no.

"I'm getting the doc," Kenny said, jumping down from the wagon before Callie could protest again.

"Morning, Kenny," Norman said as he sat drinking a cup of coffee. He lifted it up and said, "want a cup?"

"Morning," Kenny answered. "I'll get one as soon as I get back."

"Where you off to so early?" Nellie asked; she was getting the pans ready to go over the fire while Michelle mixed pancake batter. "The sun isn't even up yet."

"I wanna get Dr. Martin to come look at Callie," Kenny explained. "She's feeling poorly this morning, and I still worry about how hard she hit her head."

"What's wrong with her?" Nellie asked, becoming concerned.

"She keeps throwing up," Kenny said. "Same thing happened a few days ago. She doesn't even want to talk about food."

"I don't remember her being sick a few days ago," Nellie said.

"Once she got up and got moving, she said she felt better," Kenny said. "I'd just feel better if the doctor looked at her."

"Do you mind if I go check on her while you get him?" Nellie asked.

"Of course not," Kenny said. "You think you might know what's wrong with her?"

"Maybe," Nellie said. She took a dry biscuit left over from yesterday's supper and poured a cup of water. She turned to Michelle and asked, "you alright to finish breakfast this morning by yourself?"

"Of course," Michelle answered. "You go check on Callie and give her my love. I hope she's alright."

"I think she'll be fine," Nellie assured her.

"Eddie and I'll help Michelle," Norman offered, patting the boy who was still trying to wake up on the back, "you go look in on our girl."

Nellie walked over to the wagon Callie shared with Kenny and called into the back, "Callie, it's Mama, can I come up?"

"I'm not feeling too good this morning, Mama," Callie called back, "you might not want to get to close."

"I'll take my chances," Nellie said, climbing into the back of the wagon. "Tell Mama what's wrong?"

Callie couldn't help it; she grinned at Nellie. "I just feel terrible," she answered. "My stomach is churning, and I'm just so tired."

"Here," Nellie said, handing her the biscuit and water. "Nibble on this, I think it'll help."

"I don't know, Mama," Callie said doubtfully, taking the biscuit. She broke off a small piece and put it in her mouth.

"Callie," Nellie said seriously, "when are you due to get your next monthly?"

"I've lost track out on the trail," Callie admitted. "It's been a while since I've had it."

"Can you remember where we were on the trail the last time?" Nellie asked.

Callie thought about it, then said, "it was after we left Independence Rock, but before we got to Soda Springs."

"That's almost two months ago," Nellie said, a grin coming to her face.

"Why are you grinning, Mama?" Callie asked. "I feel horrible."

"Tell me, Callie, are your breasts tender?" Nellie asked.

Callie blushed thinking about how sensitive they seemed last night as Kenny touched them. "Yes," she finally said.

"I don't think you're sick," Nellie said, "I think you're going to have a baby."

"A baby?" Callie asked, grinning herself. "You think I'm going to be a Mama?"

"That's my guess," Nellie said, but was interrupted by Dr. Martin showing up at the wagon. They heard him tell Kenny to wait outside before he peeked into the back.

"I hear you're not feeling well, young lady," Dr. Martin said as he climbed into the wagon. "Can you tell me what's ailing you?"

"Mama thinks I'm going to have a baby?" Callie said to him.

"I can check for you if you want to know for sure," Doc Martin told her.

"Will you stay with me, Mama?" Callie asked nervously.

"Of course I will," Nellie assured her.

Ten minutes later Dr. Martin climbed out of the wagon and helped Nellie down. He motioned to Kenny that he was done, "your wife should be fine," he said to him, "but she'd like to talk to you."

"Thanks, Doc," Kenny said as he climbed into the wagon.

Norman watched him enter and turned to his wife who immediately began helping Michelle finish up breakfast. He was just about to ask what the doctor said when he heard Kenny let out an excited whoop inside the wagon.

"What's that all about?" he asked Nellie quietly so the other's wouldn't hear.

"She just told Kenny her news, Grandpa," Nellie whispered to him.

Norman nodded still confused until Nellie's words sunk in. "Grandpa?" he asked.

"Looks like it," Nellie said and had to laugh when Norman let out a whoop of his own.

**\*\*\*\*\*\*\*\*\*\***

"Callie and I want to talk to all of you about a few things," Kenny said to his and Callie's family later that night after setting up camp and eating supper.

"Is something wrong?" Henry asked.

"No," Kenny said, "for the first time in a long time, everything is right."

"Tell us, Kenny," Michelle said, "I've known all day something was going on. You and Callie off whispering, Norman and Nellie off whispering."

"First off, I want to let you all in on something only Henry and Nick know about," Kenny told them. He glanced over at Henry who nodded at him to keep going. "When we purchased the land in Oregon, we had quite a bit of money from the sale of Papa's farm. Instead of just buying three plots, Nick bought one, and I purchased seven."

"Why so many, Kenny?" Eddie asked.

"Because they were all together and there's a river that flows through the middle of the properties. I plan on giving one to each of you," Kenny explained.

"Even me?" Michelle asked.

"Even you," Kenny said. "I hope that when it comes time for you to marry, you might want to stay on it and build a house of your own."

Michelle smiled and said, "I'd like that. What about the other three?"

"I was planning on holding onto one in case Lily decides to come," Kenny said, "although I don't know how she'd get here now. I'd like to keep two for myself."

129

"There's still one more," Eddie said, doing the math in his head.

"I'd like to offer that one to Norman and Nellie," Kenny said. He turned to Norman and said, "I'll let you have it for what I paid for it."

"We accept," Norman said quickly.

"Don't you want to know what I paid for it first?" Kenny asked.

"It doesn't matter," Nellie told him, "we just want to stay close to you and Callie. We can work out the details later."

"Then that's settled," Kenny said, and Callie got up and hugged both her parents.

"All I ask from all of you is if you ever plan on selling, you offer the land to me or Henry first," Kenny said.

"I'm never selling," Michelle said, and Kenny nodded at her.

"Now for the best news," Kenny said and looked over at Callie. "Do you want to tell them?"

"You can," Callie said, her face once again turning red.

"What's going on, Kenny?" Michelle asked. "Just tell us already."

"How do you feel about becoming an aunt?" Kenny asked her. Michelle had to think for a second before she got his meaning.

"You and Callie?" she asked.

"Yep," Kenny said smiling again.

"I can't believe it," Henry said, shaking his head as he smiled back at his brother, "what a difference six months makes."

"What do you mean, Henry?" Eddie asked.

"When Mama and Papa died I didn't think any of us would ever be the same," Henry said, "but look at us now. In about two weeks we'll be in Oregon City. Michelle and you both seem happy again, and Kenny's married with a baby on the way."

"I agree, Henry," Kenny said, putting his arm around his wife and pulling her close. "When Sadie died I didn't think I'd ever be happy again. Now here I am, married to a woman I love more than I ever thought possible; and I'm about to become a Papa."

"A new Johnson," Eddie said and grinned.

"The first of many hopefully," Kenny said.

"How many?" Callie said, beginning to laugh.

"However many God decides to give us," Kenny said, holding back a laugh of his own.

"I can't wait to write a letter to Lily, Grandma and Grandpa," Michelle said, "they'll be so excited."

"I hope so," Kenny told her. "I think we should be turning in. We need our sleep. Soon we'll be in Oregon, and the real work begins."

"We'll see you young folk in the morning," Norman said, helping Nellie up and walking with her to their wagon.

"Do you think Lily's happy back in Paducah?" Michelle asked as she got up.

"I'm sure she is, she'll be marrying Jeremiah in a few weeks," Kenny said as he kissed her on the forehead. "Good night, little sister, sweet dreams."

"Good night, big brother," Michelle said, hugging first him and then Callie, "I'm so happy for you both."

Kenny watched his brothers and sister as they headed off to their wagon for the night. The difference in all of them since this trip started was incredible. Michelle smiled all the time again; although a big part of that came from the attention she got from Nellie. Eddie had reverted back to his inquisitive self, asking never-ending questions. Henry seemed to look forward to the future and couldn't wait to start building their new homestead. He knew then that his decision to bring them along on the Oregon Trail with him had been the right one.

"You ready for bed, wife?" he asked Callie, extending his hand to her.

"I don't think I'll ever get tired of hearing you say it," she said to him.

"Saying what?" he asked.

"That you love me," she said, smiling at him. "You told your whole family how much you love me."

"Because I do," he said, pulling her to him and kissing her soundly. "It may have taken me awhile to realize it, but Callie Johnson, you're the love of my life."

"You don't regret having to marry me anymore?" she asked.

"I never regretted marrying you," Kenny said as he helped her into the back of the wagon. "Getting married on the Oregon Trail was the best thing that ever happened to me."

"You sure are getting good with those words," Callie said, and she began undressing, "I think you deserve a reward."

Kenny watched as she let her dress drop to the wagon floor. He swallowed, wondering how he's gotten lucky enough to catch this wonderful woman. "A reward?" he asked. "What kind of a reward?"

"Take your clothes off, and I'll show you," Callie said, grinning at him. Kenny never got undressed so quickly in his life.

# Epilogue

"I can't believe we made it," Callie said as she grabbed hold of Kenny's arm.

"Of course we did," Kenny said to her as they rode into Oregon City.

"How long will we stay here, Kenny?" Eddie asked from the back of the wagon.

"A few days," Kenny answered. "We'll find a hotel and get a few rooms. Then tomorrow I'll find the land office and get a map to the land that I bought."

"I can't believe Mama and Papa are going to be living so close to us," Callie said. "Did I thank you for that?"

"You did," Kenny said, then leaned over and whispered, "more than once last night." Callie blushed.

"I'm just so glad," Callie said. "I'd miss them if they had to go further away."

"Is it far to your land?" Eddie asked.

"Our land, Eddie, and no, just another day or two to the southwest I think," Kenny answered. "Before we go there, I want to put in an order at one of the mills for some lumber. It'll take us a few weeks to clear the land for the houses we want to build. Hopefully, by the time we're done, our lumber order will be ready."

"What if it's not?" Eddie asked.

"We can always start Henry's log cabin," Kenny told him. "Norman and Nellie said they wouldn't mind a log cabin either. There's plenty to do to keep us busy."

"There's the post office," Eddie said pointing. "Can we stop and see if there are any letters from home?"

"I don't see why not," Kenny said and pulled the wagon in front of the building and stopped. Henry and Norman pulled their wagons over behind him.

"I'm going to go see about buying some horses," Norman said as he headed to the livery that was across the street.

"It would be nice to ride a horse again," Henry said as he got down from the wagon and stretched. He then walked into the post office with Kenny. Michelle and Eddie waited with Nellie and Callie out by the wagons.

"Can I help you?" the man behind the counter asked.

"Howdy," Kenny greeted the man. "We just arrived with a wagon train today. We gave this town as the place we'd be heading and wanted to see if there might be any mail for us."

"What's your name, son?" the postman asked.

"Kenny Johnson," he answered. "They could also be posted to Henry, Michelle or Eddie Johnson."

"Give me a second," the postman said, pulling out a box of unclaimed mail and looking through it. "We put anything that hasn't been picked up within a month in here. Most of it's mail for people coming in on the wagon trains."

"I thought there'd be a stack by now," Kenny said, a bit concerned.

"Ah," the postman finally said. "Here's one." He continued to look until he'd gone through them all. "This is the only one," he said as he handed the letter over to Kenny.

"Are you sure?" Henry asked. He too thought there would be a lot more.

"Positive," the postman said. "If you tell me where you folks will be, I'll let you know if more comes in. We get mail about once a week here."

"We'll be staying at one of the hotels for the next couple days," Kenny told him. "Then we're heading to the Willamette Valley."

"You planning on raising cattle?" the postman asked.

"We do," Kenny told him. "I'll be back in a few days to see if there might be more mail. Thanks for your help."

"Anytime," the postman answered.

Kenny and Henry walked out of the post office and over to the wagons. "Was there any letters?" Eddie asked excitedly.

"Only one," Kenny said to them, holding it up.

"Hurry up and read it," Michelle said excitedly. "I can't wait to hear what's been going on back home. I hope everyone is well."

"Give me a minute," Kenny said as he ripped the letter open. He was disappointed to find only half a page of writing. He began reading aloud:

*Dearest family,*          *April 9, 1859*

*I hope you've made it to Oregon safely and are all well. I don't want to go into reasons, but I did not marry Jeremiah. I'd rather tell you in person what he's done. By the time you read this, Grandpa, Grandma and I will also be on our way to Oregon. We had to wait until Jeremiah's trial was over, so we'll be about a month behind you. I miss you so much and look forward to seeing you all.*

*Lots of Love,*
*Lily*

"Lily's coming?" Eddie asked as soon as Kenny finished.

"That's what it says," Kenny answered.

"With Grandma and Grandpa?" Michelle asked.

"That's what Lily says," Kenny answered again as he reread the letter wanting more information.

"I wonder what Jeremiah did?" Henry asked.

"It must've been something really bad for Lily to call off the wedding and for Grandma and Grandpa to be bringing her all the way out here. We'll know soon," Kenny answered.

"I can't believe your sister is coming after all," Callie said. "I look forward to meeting her."

"How long do you think it'll take them to get here?" Eddie asked.

"The letter says they're about a month behind us," Kenny said. "I hope they all make it alright. Grandma and Grandpa are strong, but I didn't expect the trip to be as hard as it was at the end."

"They'll make it," Michelle said.

"Wasn't Nick supposed to be in a train about that time?" Henry asked. "Maybe they're traveling with him."

"I doubt it," Kenny said, "I think Lily would have mentioned if they were traveling together. I sure would feel better though if they were. Lily wouldn't want to travel with him anyway."

"Don't Lily and Nick get along?" Callie asked.

"Lily and Nick courted for a while, but it didn't end well," Kenny told her.

"All we can do is pray they get here safely," Callie said.

"You're right," Kenny agreed. "Let's get us a room and a hot meal at a restaurant. I'm sure we'll find out what happened as soon as they get here."

"You got it, big brother," Henry said, "today is the first day of our new lives."

Thank you for reading "Married on the Oregon Trail" the first book in a new series. If you have questions, comments, concerns, theories, complaints, etc.....feel free to contact me at any of the resources below.

email: bethanyhauck11@yahoo.com

Facebook: https://www.facebook.com/bethanyhauck11/

Twitter: www.twitter.com/bethanyhauck11

I'd also appreciate it if you'd leave a review on Amazon or Goodreads letting me know what you thought of the book. I read all comments and answer all emails.

Happy Reading,
Bethany

# Other Books by Bethany Hauck:
## (The McCabe Series)

### An Honest Mistake
(Jacqueline and Connor)

### A Good Man
(Ross and Angela)

### The Man of Her Dreams
(Ham and Flora)

### A Nightmare Marriage
(Fiona and Logan)

### A Man of Honor
(Alastair and Mairi)

### Her Brave Knight
(Owen and Emelia)

### Coming Soon:

### His Audacious Bride
(Eadan and Kirstie)

97749901R00080

Made in the USA
Middletown, DE
07 November 2018